Nefarious

By
Mark Stephen O'Neal

This is a work of fiction that contains imaginary names, characters, places, events and incidents not intended to resemble any actual persons, alive or dead, places, events or incidents. Any resemblances to people, places, events or incidents are entirely coincidental.

1

Mitch Black's daily routine was interrupted at the 147th East exit with a lane closure and traffic buildup all the way to the Bishop Ford Expressway split and beyond. He lived in the township of Lynwood, Illinois, a southern suburb on the outskirts of Chicago.

"Man, this is unbelievable!" Mitch shouted to himself. "Why is there road construction going on in the middle of rush hour?! Do they even care that some of us still have to go to work? Damn."

He decided to exit the expressway at Ninety-Fifth and Stony Island, instead of enduring the bumper-to-bumper traffic jam, and traveled east on Ninety-Fifth Street to Jeffery Boulevard. He hated taking side streets to work, even though he loved passing through his old neighborhood from time to time.

When he was fifteen minutes from downtown, he thought of stopping for a breakfast sandwich and coffee before work. Before the light turned green, he saw his college roommate crossing the street. He turned right on Seventy-First Street and parked his car.

"Yo, Max!" Mitch shouted, trying to get his attention. "What's up, man?"

"Black?" Max asked, looking in Mitch's direction with blood-shot eyes.

"Get in, man. I've got a few minutes to spare, and I can drop you off wherever you need to go."

"Thanks, Black, I appreciate it. So, I see you got it going on, man...got fresh chrome rims on the Benz and everything. Life must be good, huh?"

"I can't complain, Max. I got a job as a financial analyst after graduation, and I got married four years ago. We bought a house in Lynwood."

"That's good to hear, man. I'm truly happy for you."

"Where are you coming from?"

"My man Mack's spot. I got high as hell last night, so I crashed over there."

"Straight?"

"Yeah, bruh. I was pissed off because my job is trying to block my unemployment. They said I was drinking on the job...that I basically fired myself. I got drunk and smoked a bag to keep my mind off of it."

"Were you?"

"Yeah, I mean...I had a couple of beers at lunch, and someone smelled liquor on my breath. My boss found out and fired me on the spot."

"Damn, man, I sorry to hear that. So, where can I drop you off?"

"I live on South Shore Drive in the high-rise on the corner."

"I know the one. We used to stay there a couple of years ago."

"Did you? I didn't know that. I've been here a year."

"Yeah, it was our first place after college. Hey, if you need anything, let me know, okay?"

"Do you got some cash on you? If I don't pay this rent, they are going to evict me on the fifth."

"I got you covered, Max. I'm going to call my assistant and tell her that I'm running a little late. How much do you need?"

"Damn, you got an assistant...lemme hold five hundred. I'll pay you back when I get back on my feet."

"Don't even sweat that. Consider it a gift."

"Thanks again, Black. You are a true friend."

"You're welcome."

Mitch reached in his pocket and pulled out a gold money clip full of hundreds and twenties. He then took off the money clip, counted out five one-hundred-dollar bills and handed them to Max, short for Gary Maxwell, before he drove off.

Max was a slim but wiry guy who was about six feet in height, and he had a rugged look like a construction worker or a carpenter. He also had deep, sullen eyes that seemed to look directly inside a person's soul.

"Thanks, bruh. You've always had my back, and I appreciate you."

"No problem, man."

Mitch pulled up in front of the high rise about five minutes later, and Max said, "Well, this is it. Stay up, Black."

"Hey, man, wanna grab some breakfast somewhere?"

"Don't you gotta be at work?"

"Don't worry about it, bro. It's been over seven years, and we need to catch up."

"Alright, bruh, lemme tell Jill what's going on, and we can go to that waffle house off 87th and Cottage Grove."

"You and Jill are still together?"

"Yeah, we're still going strong."

"That's great, man."

Mitch dialed his cell phone and said, "Hello, Connie, something has come up, and I won't be in today. If my wife calls, tell her I'll be in meetings all day. Okay, bye."

Mitch then disconnected the call, and Max got out and went inside the high rise. A few minutes had passed before he came back outside.

"I like that waffle house spot, too," Mitch said after Max hopped back inside the car. "I took Sandra there a few times."

"You married Sandra, huh?" Max asked.

"Yeah, I brought her to Chicago after graduation, and we tied the knot a year after that."

"I can't believe a playa like you got married—I mean—you had more honeys than any guy I ever knew."

"Yeah, I've settled down a little bit, but that doesn't mean a playa don't play every now and then."

"I ain't mad at you, Black."

Mitch drove off and asked, "What about you? Did you marry Jill?"

"Yeah, and we got a baby boy," Max answered. "So, do you got any kids?"

"Nah, not yet. But it's not like I haven't been trying though—I'm beginning to think Sandra can't have any kids, or I'm shooting blanks—one or the other."

"Y'all will be aiight. You know, I wondered what happened to the whole squad once I got kicked off the basketball team and out of school. I'm glad you're livin' the dream."

"I wondered what happened to you, too. I never heard from you after that—I tried calling your mom's house in Houston, but she told me you didn't live there anymore and hung up on me."

"She kicked me out the house once TSU revoked my scholarship and kicked me out of school for selling weed."

"I'm sorry your mom did that to you, bro. I didn't play anymore after you left, either—I blew out my knee before the season ended."

"At least you graduated, bruh."

"How did you end up in Chicago?" Mitch asked, changing the subject.

"I got a cousin that stays on the west side, and once I got outta jail, I moved to Chicago and crashed at his place until I got on my feet," Max answered. "Jill followed me up here a few months after that."

"That's cool. I had no idea you were in town all this time. We definitely have to keep in touch."

"Yeah, man, and Jill would be happy to see you."

Mitch parked in the lot of the waffle house moments later, and they went inside. The hostess promptly led them to a booth by a window viewing 87th Street.

"I haven't been on this side of town in a minute," Mitch said.

"Nothing has changed," Max said. "If anything, it's gotten hotter over here since I first moved to Chicago. Seventy Ninth Street is just like the 'ho stroll on Madison Avenue."

"That's messed up, man. This used to be a thriving community growing up."

"That was then."

The server brought their food to the table—Mitch had bacon, eggs and grits, and Max ordered a waffle and sausages. Mitch also ordered an orange juice, and Max stuck with water.

"What you got going on later?" Mitch asked.

"Nothing much," Max answered. "Me and Jill gotta take Gary Jr. to the clinic this afternoon."

"Is he sick?"

"Nah, I don't think so. He might have a slight cold, but you can never be too careful."

"Indeed. So, you named him after you, huh?"

"Yeah, that's my little man."

"That's what's up."

"What you got going on since you're playing hooky?"

"I don't know—maybe I'll hit up my girl, Jada. She should be in class right now, though."

"One of your honeys?"

"Yeah, you can say that."

"Same old Black."

They finished up their food, and Mitch paid the bill and tipped the server handsomely.

"You want me to drop you back off at your apartment?" Mitch asked.

"Nah, you can drop me back off at my boy Mack's crib," Max answered. "I gotta hammer out some biz with him before I take Junior to the clinic."

"Where does he stay?"

"A few blocks from here on 87th and Indiana."

"Okay."

Mitch parked in front of Mack's apartment complex a few minutes later. Mitch handed Max one of his business cards and said, "Call me if you ever need anything, and write your number on the back of this card."

"That's what's up, Black," Max said. "I'll holla at you later."

"Peace, my brother."

Max got out and went inside the apartment complex, and Mitch drove off. It was now late morning, so he decided to head up to the DePaul University campus in Lincoln Park to find Jada.

2

Mitch found a convenient spot to park near campus, so he could wait for Jada to finish class. He texted her and waited for her to call or text back. Fifteen minutes later, his cell phone rang.

"Hey, Jada, how are you?" he asked.

"I'm fine, baby," she answered. "I just got out of class. Is everything okay?"

"Everything's cool. Can you meet me for lunch?"

"Sure, baby. Where?"

"I'm right here on campus."

"Where exactly?"

"I can meet you wherever you're at."

"Meet me at the corner of Sheffield and Fullerton."

"Okay, see you in a few minutes."

He ended the call and drove to the location where she told him to go. Jada Sims attended DePaul University at the Northside campus, and she was studying for her master's in journalism. Her dream was to write for the Chicago Sun-Times and eventually become a news anchor for a major network, and she was definitely photogenic.

Mitch met Jada in high school, and they dated senior year. They were each other's first love, and she waited until prom night to lose her virginity with him. Their experience wasn't anything like the movies—there weren't any fireworks or ecstasy before, during, or after their first encounter because he was too focused on not hurting her, instead of making sure that they both enjoyed the experience. Even though their first night together was less than stellar, the bond between them became stronger. However, fate would inevitably break them up when he got accepted at Texas Southern University, and she got a full ride to Illinois State because she scored a 27 on the ACT. They tried to maintain a long-distance relationship but failed after the first year. She started dating a basketball player, and he met Sandra, his wife, at TSU.

He arrived at the designated location, and she was standing on the corner in front of the DePaul University sign. He pulled over to the side of the street and put on his hazard lights. She got in moments later and kissed him on the lips.

"I missed you so much," she said. "This is such a pleasant surprise."

"I missed you, too, Jada," he said. "What do you have a taste for?"

"Ooh, can we go to Ruth Chris?"

"Damn, you must think I'm a baller or something."

"What, you ain't good for it?"

"I'm just playing, baby. You can have anything you want."

"I already got what I want."

"Oh yeah, what's that?"

"Your heart, silly," she answered, punching him lightly on the arm.

He smiled and said, "You're right, you do have my heart. I just have to figure out a way to tell Sandra."

"Well, don't take too much longer because I want to start a family someday."

"I promise I won't."

They arrived at the restaurant, and he handed the valet the keys. They got their table and ordered some appetizers and drinks. Jada looked Mitch in his eyes and said, "So, you decided to get an early start on the weekend by slumming on a Friday afternoon, huh? I love your company and all, but what's really going on?"

"Don't trip, sweetheart. I didn't lose my job. I ran into Gary Maxwell today..."

"Who, your teammate from college?"

"Yeah, and he's married with a newborn son."

"Wow, that's great. Where did you run into him?"

"On my way to work. Traffic was murder on I-94, so I took Jeffery on down to the lakefront, and that's when I saw him walking down 71st Street. He was on his way to his apartment on South Shore Drive when I picked him up."

"Let me guess—you decided to ditch work, so you two could catch up, right?"

"Bingo, you guessed it. It was cool, Jada, real cool seeing him again. We had breakfast at that spot off 87th and Cottage Grove."

"The one next to the car wash and across the street from the Seaway Bank—I've been there once or twice."

"Yeah, the food there is decent, too."

"You seem real excited about hanging out with him."

"You know, I always wondered what happened to him after he got kicked out of school. He was my best friend..."

"What's he up to nowadays?"

"He just lost his job, so I gave him five hundred dollars to cover his rent for the month."

"You haven't seen this guy in what, seven years, and you gave him five hundred dollars?"

"I know where you're going with this, and it's not like that."

"I'm not going anywhere with it, baby. Just be careful, okay?"

"I will; don't worry."

"So, does Sandra know you took the day off?"

"Hell no, and the last thing I need is her accusing me of messing around on her again."

"You two are still fighting?"

"Yeah, almost every day. I know she suspects that I'm cheating on her, even though she can't prove it. Our situation isn't getting any better."

"I think we've covered our tracks pretty well, but you can never underestimate a woman, Mitch."

"I'm going to tell her it's over this weekend. We're not even going to make it to five years of being married."

"It's not meant to be, baby. Love isn't supposed to hurt, and from what you told me about her, she all wrong for you anyway. You need someone who's kind and considerate, and she's a princess who's stuck on herself."

"I got caught up in her looks before really getting to know her. Before I knew it, I was in over my head."

"It's a good thing you all don't have any kids. She would take you to the bank for sure."

"She's going to take me to the bank anyway. I make way more money than she does, and I'm definitely going to have to pay alimony."

"Hire a good lawyer—she has no grounds to come hard at you, and we don't live in a communal property state."

"I know your right, but it's not going to be that simple. She's not gonna make it easy because this is what I want. She will fight me tooth and nail."

"You can do this, and I will be with you every step of the way. I love you so much, Mitch."

He leaned over and kissed her softly on the lips. He then gazed in her beautiful brown eyes and said, "Okay, I'll definitely take care of it this weekend. You give me the strength to want to go through with it."

They continued to talk about their future and enjoy each other's company. The server brought their entrees and more drinks, and before they knew it, a couple of hours had passed. Mitch subsequently paid the waiter and took Jada to work. She was a shift manager at a check-processing center for a bank nearby and had worked there since finishing undergrad.

He pulled up in front of her building and parked. She kissed him on the cheek and got out, and he watched her walk inside before his phone rang.

"Hello?"

"When are you coming to pick me up?" Sandra asked.

He smiled and said, "I'll be there at four like we discussed, baby."

3

Gary Maxwell sat on his friend's sofa with one hand on his crotch and the other holding a Newport. Moments later, his partner in crime, Tyrone Mack, came out of his room and sat across from him. Max then reached over and handed Tyrone a cigarette from his pack and slouched back down on the sofa. Tyrone lit the cigarette with his lighter and took a puff.

Tyrone was a rather large individual—six feet, four inches tall and about two hundred fifty pounds. He was the strong, silent type who was not to be messed with.

"You ran into your boy Mitch, huh?" Tyrone asked.

"Yeah, and it was good seeing him, too," Max answered. "He helped a brother out with some cash to cover this rent."

"That's what's up."

"My man is really doing the damn thing, Mack. The hell with this nine-to-five BS, bruh—we need a score in the worst way."

"How cool are you with Mitch? Maybe we can rob him..."

"Absolutely not, homeboy. He's like a brother to me."

"You know the rules, bruh—if he ain't crew or family, he's fair game."

"I'm gonna have to pull rank on this one. Mitch is off limits, understood?"

"Aiight, man, it's cool."

Tyrone paused and said, "I know of a card game we can hit up."

"Yeah?" Max asked, rising up from the sofa. "When and where?"

"Right off seventy-ninth and Coles tonight. We could clear at least ten grand from the card game alone, and all the cash and cocaine that we can carry because it's a dope spot."

"Dope spot? Who are we robbing?"

"This bum I used to work for. I'll give you all of the details later."

"Aiight, then. Grab Norris, and we will chop it up at my place at nine. I'm out."

"Aiight, Max, peace."

"Later, Mack."

Max left, and Tyrone sat on his sofa and smiled and imagined himself living in a ten-room mansion with a swimming pool. He also thought about the 2018 Benz he was going to buy off the lot with cash.

"We're about to blow up!" Tyrone shouted to himself.

4

Mitch and Sandra rode in the direction of home in silence. They would ordinarily ride to work together every morning, as they both started work at ten, but Sandra had to be at work two hours earlier to do a coffee and water setup for an eight o'clock deposition. She took an Uber to the Metra train station, so she wouldn't disrupt Mitch's morning routine.

Mitch was in deep thought about running into Max earlier and his ongoing, torrid affair with Jada, and Sandra was still heated from getting into it with the human resource manager. She failed to inform one of the attorneys about a scheduled meeting with an important client, and she handed in her resignation before the company fired her. She was a receptionist at a downtown law firm and hated her job with a passion. Her degree was in finance, but she couldn't land a job in her field and got complacent doing what she despised for five years. Mitch had suggested she resign and look for something that made her happy, but she would consistently blow off his advice. Her philosophy was that some money was better than no money, even though Mitch paid all the household bills and mortgage, and she was free to do whatever she pleased with her check.

She turned toward Mitch and said, "What happened to you today? I called and called, but your secretary said you were in meetings all day."

"I *was* in meetings all day like she said," he lied. "Contrary to what you might think, what I do is actually important."

Sandra sighed and said, "You could've at least called me back. What if I was in an accident or something?"

"You're right, baby, and I'm sorry. I really didn't have time for much of anything today."

"I was calling you because I took your advice and put in my two-week notice today. I'm gonna go back to school for my master's."

Mitch stared straight ahead and didn't pay attention to Sandra's comment. He was thinking about hooking up with Jada later on that night.

"Did you hear what I said?" she asked.

"What? Yeah, I heard you. No sense in staying somewhere when you're not happy."

"I agree, baby. Let's go somewhere and get something to eat."

"Sure, where do you want to go?"

"I have a taste for some seafood. What about Red Lobster?"

"Okay, Red Lobster is fine."

"Can we take a trip? Maybe Cancun or the Bahamas?"

"When, baby?"

"How about this weekend?"

"This month isn't good because I have a ton of stuff to do at work and at the club, but we can go next month for sure."

"Okay, that's fine. I'll make the reservations tonight."

"Good, I'm looking forward to this. I love you, Sandra, and I support you one hundred percent."

"I love you, too, and I can wait to escape for a few days."

They arrived at Red Lobster about forty-five minutes later and ordered over a hundred dollars' worth of appetizers, entrees, drinks and desserts. A couple of hours had passed before Mitch got the check and tipped the server, and they went home. They weren't in the house five seconds when Sandra grabbed Mitch's crotch and shoved her tongue down his throat. He picked up her petite five-foot-two-inch frame moments later and carried her off to the bedroom. Sandra had flawless chocolate-colored skin and a shapely, athletic body. However, her best attribute was her radiant smile that had captured Mitch's heart from the start in college.

They indulged in heated passion until both of them lay flat on their backs, sweaty and completely satisfied. Mitch reached for his pants and grabbed his pack of cigarettes afterward, and Sandra handed him a lighter from the nightstand and lit his cigarette for him. He then took a puff and blew smoke out of his nostrils.

"I really needed that," he said. "It's been a long week."

"Me, too, baby," she said. "You're my favorite stress reliever. My treadmill comes in a distant second."

He kissed her on the forehead and got out of bed. He reached for his pants and said, "I'm about to run out for a little while. Do you want me to bring you something back?"

"No, and where do you think you're going this late?" she asked, raising her eyebrows.

"Relax, baby. I told Wes I'd meet him at the club later on tonight. It's just business."

"Well, you could've told me sooner. I know y'all got a business to run but give me a heads-up next time. I thought we were going to spend the rest of the night together."

"I'll make it up to you, baby, I promise. Don't worry, we're gonna pick up where we left off when I get back."

"And if I'm sleep, you better wake mama up for her dessert."

5

Mitch had taken a few minutes to freshen up before heading out to the club. He really did have some business to take care with his cousin, Wesley, but he didn't give full disclosure of the entire truth. He had planned on spending a half hour or forty-five minutes tops discussing weekly profits and more money-laundering schemes to hide Wesley's drug money, then it was off to Jada's house for some quick nooky.

He had been keeping up the lie for about two years, and even though things with Sandra were good, the playa in him wanted to have his cake and eat it too. He knew that the only way he could get in Jada's pants was to say that his marriage was on the rocks. However, Jada was getting restless and wanted more of a commitment soon.

Mitch opened up *Club Ecstasy* with Wesley a year ago in Bridgeview, a southwestern suburb of Chicago. It caught on like wildfire—so much so that Wesley was able to get out of the drug game for good—but not without complications. Wesley's rival, Cedric Nash, was pissed at him for giving up his connection to his right-hand man, Flip, without cutting him in on it.

Wesley was tired of getting ripped off by the mob and decided to deal with one of the Mexican cartels a few months before opening up the club. He went straight to Tijuana and garnered a deal that would allow him to undercut Cedric's price and move into the number one spot on the south side of town. He had learned Spanish from his girlfriend Marisol, who's Puerto Rican, so setting up a deal wasn't very difficult. The truce that he had established with Cedric was broken, and they had been feuding ever since then. Wesley would sometimes have to wear a bulletproof vest and would always stay strapped whenever he left home from that point on.

The club was packed as usual, with a long line to get in, when Mitch arrived. It wasn't quite twelve o'clock yet, and he wanted to be in and out as quickly as possible before indulging in his second nightcap. He surveyed the front of the club and the parking lot before finding a spot nearby. He studied a beautiful young woman wearing an outlandish, tight-fitting green and purple dress with matching green go-go boots that came up to her knees before stepping out of the car. She returned his stare with a smile as she continued to walk toward the line that now wrapped around the corner.

He tossed his cigarette on the ground and put it out with his shoe. He then walked toward entrance and greeted Sam at the door.

"Another packed night," Mitch said. "Business is good."

"It's been like this all week, boss," Sam said. "We're the hottest ticket in town."

"Where's Wes?" Mitch asked.

"He's waiting for you in VIP," Sam answered.

Mitch gave Sam some dap and went inside. The crowd stared as he walked toward the bar and greeted the bartender and two barmaids. Biggie's old school cut *Juicy* was playing as he made his way toward VIP. He was the object of most women and the envy of most men. He commanded respect whenever he entered a room—and if being light skinned wasn't in anymore, one couldn't tell by the flock of women he attracted with ease. He was extremely confident and comfortable in any setting, and this was mistaken for being arrogant more often than not. In spite of that fact, he was still a very likable person.

He was moderately tall—slightly over six feet—with broad shoulders and an athletic build. He also had big hands and feet—another trait women loved about him. He was the type of guy that looked good in any clothes he had on, and he definitely made the outfit, not the other way around.

Mitch opened the door and found Wesley conversing with two beautiful women. He noticed Mitch and whispered something to them. Both women got up and left the room afterwards.

Wesley stood up and gave Mitch a hug and said, "What took you so long, cuz?"

"I got tied up, man," Mitch answered. "The woman of the house wanted to dine out tonight."

"That's cool."

"I ran into Max this morning, and we hung out for breakfast at that wafflc house off 87th and Cottage."

"Yeah? What's he doing in Chicago?"

"He's been living here since he got kicked out of TSU."

"Really? Don't get caught up in his nonsense, Mitch. I don't trust him, and I never have."

"That's not fair, Wes. I never judge the lowlifes you associate with."

"Lowlifes come with the territory, college boy."

"Whatever, man. So, how are we looking this month?"

"We're looking great. If things keep going like this, we'll be able to open another spot—maybe one in Harvey or something. I would open one in Chicago, but it's too much red tape and politics to deal with."

"I don't know about that, man. I think we should diversify, you know, maybe open a barbershop or carwash. Clubs don't always stay hot, but people will always need haircuts or to get their cars washed."

"You're right, cuz, and that's why you're my partner."

Mitch glanced at the bottle of Crown Royal on the table, and he walked over to the mini-bar to get a glass. He poured himself a shot and gulped it down.

"Whew, I needed that," Mitch said. "Who were those girls in here a minute ago?"

"I interviewed some dancers earlier this week, and they were the last two I hired," Wesley answered.

"Good. That's gonna bring in even more money, especially during weeks when it's a little slow. Thursday would be the perfect day to have them dance."

"That's a good idea. I was thinking Wednesday and Thursday, but we can have a test run on Thursdays for a month to see how things go."

"Alright, cool. I'm out, Wes."

"Where are you going, man? You just got here."

"I'm hooking up with Jada. I gotta get in where I fit in."

"Your creepin' is gonna be the death of you one day, man. See you later."

"Peace."

Wesley Hunter poured himself a shot and gulped it. He had the quickest pair of hands in the neighborhood growing up, and nobody ever thought about crossing him. He was three years older than Mitch, and he always thought of Mitch like a younger brother, whom he protected from the various thugs and bullies who tried to pick fights with him. He had once gotten into a fight over a pick-up game of basketball in the seventh grade with an older kid from the neighboring high school. He more than held his own as the crowd gathered around them, and he ended up breaking the guy's nose and knocking out his two front teeth. After that, his reputation was born.

He looked down at the crowd on the dance floor and smiled. He had turned his life around, and things couldn't be sweeter. Contrary to his cousin's lifestyle, he was faithful to his girlfriend of five years, and they had a son together. Things were good between them, and he had given serious thought to proposing to her now that he wasn't hustling anymore.

He picked up his phone and dialed home.

"Hey, baby, it me," Wesley said. "How my little man?"

"He's sound asleep, sweetheart," Marisol answered. "Sounds like it's packed in there."

"It's a full house. Will you wait up for me? I'll be there about three."

"Yes, I'll be here waiting for you. I cooked your favorite."

"Okay, baby, see you then."

"Bye."

He hung up the phone and poured a full glass of Crown Royal. He continued to sit in VIP alone and didn't feel like socializing with anybody. In fact, the club was originally Mitch's idea because it was his natural habitat, while Wesley never really felt comfortable around crowds of people. Mitch would literally pick up a different girl every night, while Wesley was more reserved and picky about his choice of a woman.

He was in deep thought and was shaken when one of his bouncers entered the room.

"Everything okay, Wes?" the bouncer asked.

"Yeah, I'm cool," he answered. "What's up?"

"We might have a little situation at the door. Some guys are getting loud and unruly because they aren't dressed right, and I wouldn't let them in."

"Come on. Let's go diffuse this BS."

6

When Wesley and the bouncer got downstairs to the entrance of the club, Mitch had already handled the situation. He was standing by the end of the bar closest to the door talking to one of the other bouncers and one of the barmaids. There didn't appear to be any type of disturbance whatsoever.

"What the hell happened down here, Mitch?" Wesley asked.

"Everything's cool, Wes," Mitch answered. "Some guys weren't appropriately dressed, and they were a little upset about not being able to get in. I gave them some free-drink vouchers for the next time they come, and they calmed down and left."

"Good looking out, Mitch," Wesley said. "I like the way you handled that because I would've just kicked them outta here."

"Man, you really need to improve your people skills," Mitch said. "The last thing we need is a shootout up here."

"And like I said before, that's why I'm in business with you," Wesley said.

Mitch looked in the direction of the dance floor and locked in on a drop-dead gorgeous woman with a caramel complexion sitting in one of the chairs at the other end of the bar, and Toni Braxton's song "Long as I Live" was playing in the background. She was wearing a black cat suit and black stilettos, and her hair was long and silky. She turned her head and met Mitch's gaze head-on—they were like two boxers sizing each other up at the weigh-in.

Although Mitch had more than he could handle with Sandra, who was a cocoa-brown athletic beauty, and Jada, who was five feet, six inches of voluptuous caramel, this woman's body measurements were illegal. The look in her eyes revealed a hint of pernicious intent behind her angelic face, and a wise man would definitely approach her with extreme caution. She was so sexy that she was dangerous—like the thrill and rush of driving 120 miles per hour on the expressway with ever-present state troopers lurking in the shadows.

But Mitch let greed get the best of him, and he wasn't short on confidence when it came to the opposite sex. Women were a sport to him, and this woman was no exception. Mitch's rule was always to tell a girl he was married but never tell her he had a mistress. In his mind, a girl may play the second position, but she may not be willing to play the third spot.

Mitch walked up to where she was sitting and said, "Excuse me, sexy, I just can't leave here without saying something to you."

"Oh, yeah," she said, "what is this 'something' you want to say to me?"

"That you are the most beautiful woman I've ever seen in my life, and I want to get to know you better," Mitch answered.

She blushed and said, "Boy, how many times have you used that line?"

"I promise you that what I say is straight from the heart, and I've never said that to any other woman. You-are-breathtaking."

"Thank you."

"Mitch—my name is Mitch, and you are?"

"I'm Brea."

"Nice to meet you."

"Likewise."

"Look, I'm gonna just put it all out here—I'm married, and I own this club with my cousin. I don't do this sort of thing every day, but there's something about you, Brea."

"I'm not gonna front, either, Mitch. I only deal with men who are attached to somebody already, and they have to pay to play, hon. What I don't need is some guy trying to spend *all* his free time with me, so if you're game, you can start by buying me a cup of coffee somewhere."

"Okay, Brea, you have a deal. Let's get out of here—we can take my car."

They then left the club together, and Mitch walked a few steps behind Brea after saying goodbye to Wesley and Sam at the door. Her strut mesmerized him as they sauntered toward his car. She appeared to be about five-foot-seven or eight, but it was hard to tell with her heels on. She had legs for days, an ample derriere, and a bosom that would make Dolly Parton jealous.

"Where's your car?" Brea asked.

"The white Benz over there," Mitch replied, pointing to the left of them.

"Damn, boy, are you a drug dealer?"

"What, a brother can't be successful?"

"I'm just saying, my ex has a car like this, and let's just say that he keeps most of the fiends happy on the south side."

Mitch disarmed the alarm on his car, opened and shut Brea's door for her, and trotted to the driver's side door and got in. It was still warm outside from a humid June day, so he let down the windows.

"Well, for starters, I'm not a drug dealer, Brea. I graduated at the top of my class at TSU, got married, and I'm a financial analyst by day."

"You went to Texas Southern?"

"Yeah, why?"

"I went to Texas Southern, too."

"Get outta here! When? I'm sure I would have remembered you."

"I just finished my first year, and I just got back home a few weeks ago. Once I broke up with my ex, I figured I'd give school a try. I went to TSU afterwards and majored in art, but I'm probably not going back."

"Why not?" he said, scratching his head.

She frowned and said, "School isn't for me. I want to sing, and I'm going to shop my demo to every record label I can."

"You can sing, huh? Bust a note for me."

"What? Hell no, boy. I'll sing for you when I know you better."

"I get it—you're shy, right? I understand."

"I-am-not-shy, Mitch," she said, waving her index finger with each syllable in his face.

"Lemme hear you sing then, Miss Sassy. Please?"

"Oh, alright."

She sang a verse from the classic song "Real Love" by Mary J. Blige, and she sang like an angel. Mitch certainly thought she sounded as good as she looked.

"Damn girl, you got mad skills. Don't forget about me when you blow up."

"I won't."

Brea observed the interior of Mitch's car—the plush white leather seats, the state-of-the-art sound system, and his cell phone. She smiled and said, "You got the iPhone 8, huh?"

"Yeah, I just bought it last week."

"I had one similar to that one, but my ex took it back when we broke up."

"Somebody was crazy enough to leave you? Why?"

She blushed again and said, "He tried to control my every move, and I wasn't down with that. He has a wife, too, and he expected me to be at his beckoned call like she was. He broke the rules of our relationship by getting too caught up in my life, so I had to step off."

"Did you love him?"

"Yes, I did, but feelings change. What about you? Do you love your wife?"

"I'm not gonna lie," he lied. "I do, but I'm not in love with her anymore. Seeing you tonight reminded me of that fact."

"Oh, really?" she said in a skeptical tone.

"Yes, you're what I've been searching for my whole life. You are absolutely gorgeous, Brea."

"Thank you, but you don't even know me."

"I know what I feel, and I want to know everything I can about you."

"I want to get to know you, too."

Mitch leaned in and kissed Brea softly on her lips. She didn't stop him, and she gently caressed the back of his head with her long, sensuous fingernails. She pulled back moments later and gazed into his eyes.

"You taste so sweet," Mitch said.

"So do you," Brea said. "You can tell a lot about a man by the way he kisses. If he can't kiss, I don't want anything else to do with him."

"So, did I pass the test?"

"Yes, baby, you passed. You can give me an encore later."

"I most definitely will. So, how old are you, if you don't mind me asking? You seem very mature for an eighteen or nineteen-year-old just finishing up her first year of college."

"Well, I'm certainly not eighteen or nineteen—my lightbulb moment didn't happen right away. I'm twenty-five."

"Wow, I'm twenty-seven. We are perfect for each other."

"Actually, sweetie, you're younger than most of the men I date. Most guys your age can't afford me, but I'll make an exception for you."

"Well, how old is your ex?"

"He's forty."

"Damn, I see you like to date senior citizens. He's about a year away from collecting Social Security."

"You got jokes, huh?"

"Yeah, I got a few."

Mitch paused and said, "There's restaurant that I like about a mile from here, and they have the best cheesecake. Is that okay with you?"

"Yes, that's fine."

Mitch finally decided to leave the parking lot and entered the main street. His phone rang shortly afterwards, but he let it go to voicemail. Jada was expecting him, but he decided to blow her off and hang with Brea instead.

"Aren't you going to answer that?" she asked. "I wouldn't want to get you in trouble with your wife because of me."

"Nah, it's cool," he answered. "I'll see her when I get home. I'm all about you right now."

"Well, in that case, let's continue to enjoy each other's company."

7

Max, Tyrone, and Norris parked at a convenience store a block away from the house where the card game was going on. Tyrone explained that he used to serve crack for the guy hosting it, and he wanted some payback for not being properly compensated for taking all the risk of slinging on the corners. Tyrone had to give a good portion of what he made back to him, and he wanted to settle the score.

Tommy Glenn, or Tommy G for short, was a low-level drug dealer on the far southeast side, who loved to flaunt his ill-gotten wealth with lots of jewelry, candy-paint traps, and high stakes poker games every Friday. His predictability proved to be Tyrone's golden opportunity to cash in on the dream that he'd been denied in his mind for so long.

Tyrone looked at Max and said, "I'm gonna quarterback this thing, and every move we make has to be precise. These guys are some trigger-happy nut jobs that shoot first and ask questions later. We're going to kill 'em all eventually, but don't shoot Tommy G unless you have to."

"Who's Tommy G?" Norris asked.

"He's the top dog," Tyrone answered, "and he's gonna lead us to the cash and the dope."

"What's the plan then, Mack?" Max asked.

"First, I want you to find a good spot about a block away from here to park, so no one can recognize the car or get a plate number," Tyrone answered.

"We can park on Coles past Eightieth Street," Norris suggested.

"Nah, don't park directly on Coles," Tyrone said. "Park in the middle of Eightieth Street between Coles and South Shore Drive."

"Parking is the least of our worries," Max stated. "Our main concern is getting in and out of the spot without anyone noticing anything. But if we have to shoot our way outta here, we want the car to be as close as possible. We can just burn the car afterward because it's a scrap heap with bogus plates that's not even worth a tank of gas."

"Let's just grab that open spot a half-block down," Tyrone said.

"Okay," Max said.

Max drove off from the store and parked in the spot that Tyrone suggested on the north side of 79th Street and a block before the railroad crossing on Exchange Avenue. Tommy G's house was two houses from the corner of 79th and Coles.

"Aiight," Tyrone said, "that part of the plan is settled. Lemme outta here, and I'll distract them for a while with my standup routine. I should've been a comedian, you know."

"Just try not to put them asleep," Max said.

"Whatever, man," Tyrone said, handing a key to Max. "Here's the back door key to the crib. I made a copy when Tommy G wasn't looking."

"Cool," Norris said. "Give us about ten minutes to scope the block and creep in through the back door."

"And if anybody reaches for their waist, blast them with a quickness," Tyrone said. "Aiight, I'm out."

"Wait," Max said.

"What's up?" Tyrone asked.

"Go to my trunk and grab the Nike bag," Max answered. "We can put the cash and dope in the bag—leave it on the back porch for us, Mack."

"What's this in the bag?" Tyrone asked.

"Latex gloves," Max answered. "We can't afford to leave fresh fingerprints anywhere."

"It's only two pair in there," Tyrone said.

"Here, take my driving gloves," Max said. "You can't walk in there with latex gloves on, anyway."

"Good lookin' out," Tyrone said.

"We can burn this piece of junk at the Forest Preserve exit off the Bishop Ford Expressway," Max instructed. "I'll have Jill meet us over there."

Tyrone got out of the car, put on the driving gloves, and walked toward the back of the house with the Nike bag. Max sent Jill a text instructing her where to meet them, and Max and Norris waited.

Norris Adams was Tyrone's younger cousin and the younger brother of Tyrone's cousin, Quentin. Norris was an intelligent, but degenerate, twenty-two-year old who loved the fast buck and would do just about anything to get it.

"Shoot first, ask questions later if any of them get outta line," Norris said.

"Absolutely," Max said. "We need one more big score, so we can stop doing this. These streets are timing us, and everyone in the game has an expiration date at some point."

"I feel you, Max, and that's why I'm gonna start my own business soon. I need to put my carpentry skills to use."

"That's what's up, Norris. I'm gonna skip town and open up a barbershop somewhere."

"Sounds like a plan."

"No doubt."

8

Mitch and Brea arrived at the restaurant, and there was a moderate crowd, even in the wee hours of the night. Mitch opened her car door for her, and they walked hand in hand to the entrance of the restaurant. He then told the hostess to give them a booth once they got inside.

The hostess led them to the back of the diner, and Mitch sat next to Brea instead of sitting across from her. A waitress brought them their menus, and he knew what he wanted and said, "You ready to order, Brea?"

"Yes, baby," she said. "Just give me a cup of coffee."

"And you, sir?" the waitress asked.

"I'll have a slice of cheesecake and a glass of milk."

"Thank you," the waitress said. "I'll take your menus."

"Milk?" Brea laughed.

"Yeah, so," Mitch answered. "What's wrong with that?"

"Nothing, I guess. Milk and liquor don't really mix, but if you like it, I love it."

"You're right, but I got a strong stomach."

"You're a better person than I am. My stomach would be in knots if I even thought about drinking some milk."

"Lactose intolerant?"

"Yeah, you can say that. Let's just say I didn't eat too many bowls of Lucky Charms or ice cream growing up."

"Damn, that's too bad, baby. You must have had some childhood."

"It's wasn't too bad—at least I got to enjoy eating cookies and cake."

"Not too much I see—it didn't ruin your beautiful smile."

She smiled and said, "Flattery will get you everywhere, young man."

She leaned in for kiss, and they gave each other a little tongue action the second time around. Mitch loved the smell of Brea's perfume and her soft, full lips, and a spark was ignited inside of Brea once his tongue met hers. They both pulled back after about a minute or so and smiled at each other.

"I can get used to a guy like you, Mitch," she said. "I'll keep you happy as long as you keep me happy. It's not just about the material things, but material things get you in the door."

"I love your honesty, Brea," he said. "Most girls aren't upfront about how they really feel. I can respect that."

"Good. I just want us to be on the same page, and FYI, we're not having sex tonight. You'll get some on the fifth date if you're still around."

"I'll be around, and I'll be looking forward to it."

"Oh, so you think so, huh?"

"I think I have a good shot."

"We'll see."

The waitress brought them their orders and asked if they needed anything else. Mitch turned to face Brea and asked, "Are you sure you don't want anything else?"

"No thanks, I'm fine," she answered.

"Yes, you are," he said.

The waitress smiled and said, "Just holla if you need me."

The waitress went back to the kitchen area, and Brea took a sip of her coffee.

"You don't put cream or sugar in your coffee?" he asked.

"Nah, I like it black," she answered. "I like all of my drinks strong—no coke with my rum and no orange juice with my vodka."

"My kind of girl."

Mitch took a bite of his cake and asked, "Wanna a bite? It's really fresh."

"No thanks, baby."

"What's your last name, Brea?"

"It's Jones. And yours?"

"Black. Now that we've been formally introduced, are you originally from Chicago?"

"Nope. I moved here about five years ago from New York."

"Yeah? Never would've guessed that. I've been in Chicago most of my life, except when I went away to school."

"I grew up in Brooklyn. My parents died two months apart from each other, and I've been on my own ever since."

"Damn, baby, I'm sorry to hear that."

"It's okay—both of them died of AIDS. My father was a heroin user, and he infected my mom. Watching them die like that was the most painful thing I'd ever experienced."

"I can't imagine, Brea. I'm so sorry."

"It was tough being without them, but I got through it. I started stripping shortly afterwards, and I did that until I was about twenty. I saved enough money to move here, and that's when I met my ex."

"How long were y'all together?"

"Almost four years. I have no regrets though, and I learned a lot from him."

"My cousin and I were raised in the same house, so we're more like brothers than anything else. My mother and grandmother raised us, and I never met my father."

"What about your cousin's parents?"

"My cousin—Wesley's mother was a junkie, and his father was killed in a drive-by shooting. His mother and my mother were sisters."

"Oh, I'm sorry to hear that."

"That's life, baby."

"You said Wesley's mom was a junkie?"

"Yeah, she died when I was six and Wesley was nine. My uncle George, my mom's oldest brother, ran the family business, and my aunt Ruth got hooked on heroin because of it. Uncle George is doing a life sentence for murder and drug trafficking."

"Wow, you come from some family. I see we have a lot in common—nobody could ever say we grew up with a normal childhood."

"That's true, but we're strong and still standing."

They talked for a while longer before he paid the waitress, and he took Brea back to the club to get her car. He parked alongside her 2018 black convertible Mustang once they got back. The club was about to close, as it was quickly approaching two o'clock in the morning.

"This car is definitely you," he said. "I love it."

"Thank you," she said. "Here's my card. You can call me anytime."

"I surely will."

They tightly embraced and kissed passionately for a brief moment before pulling back and staring into each other's eyes. He lightly pecked her on the lips and said, "I'm in love with you already, Brea."

"I promise I will be worth the wait, baby," she whispered in his ear before kissing him on the lips and getting in her car.

"I'll call you tomorrow," he said after acquiescing to the reality that their date was over.

She drove off, and Mitch stood motionless for a couple of minutes. He was already mesmerized and was in too deep from the opening gun. He then hopped in his car and drove off. He totally forgot about Jada after he ignored her call, and he fantasized about Brea the entire drive home.

He got another call from Jada when he was ten minutes away from home. He turned off the radio and picked up on the fourth ring.

"I'm sorry, baby," he said.

"What happened to you?" she asked. "I thought you were coming by."

"I know—I got tied up at the club. We had a couple of drunk patrons we had to kick out and some other issues. I promise I'll make it up to you."

"It's okay, I understand. We can get together some other time."

"I'll call you when I'm free, okay?"

"Okay. I love you, and I'll talk to you later."

"Love you, too. Bye."

He disconnected the call and continued to drive without the radio on. He felt guilty about lying to Jada and knew deep down that their relationship was about to end soon. Any free time he had from that point on now belonged to Brea. He never believed in love at first sight until that night, and after his encounter with her, his life changed instantly.

However, his wife Sandra was a different story. She would always have a part of his heart, no matter what happened with Brea. She was with him when he didn't have a pot to piss in, and he would never leave her because of that fact. Brea was the woman of his dreams, but Sandra was the love of his life. He was now torn between the two women, and he realized that taking care of home and Sandra's needs was still his number one priority, even though Brea was now his burning desire.

9

Norris scanned the perimeter for cops and potential onlookers while Max puffed on a cigarette. They stood in front of Tommy G's crack house a few minutes later and paused. Max blew some smoke out of his nose, tossed his cigarette in the street, and said, "You ready to get this money, homeboy?"

"Yeah, let's do it," Norris answered. "I'm gonna bust on anybody that blinks with this *Nina*."

They crept to the back of house and onto the back porch. Tyrone had placed the Nike bag on the right side of the back door in the corner of the porch, and Max reached inside the bag and pulled out the two pairs of latex gloves.

"Here, put these on," Max whispered. "Don't touch nothing yet."

"Okay," Norris whispered back. "How many people do you think are in there?"

"Don't know but follow my lead."

Norris racked the slide of his 9 mm, and Max pulled out his .380 semi-automatic. Max turned the key in the door slowly and opened it. They could hear the music and chatter in the living room area when entering the kitchen. Max then placed the bag on the floor and turned back toward Norris and nodded. They both stormed into the living room with their guns cocked seconds later.

"Everybody put your damn hands in the air!" Max shouted. "Nobody move!"

"Put your hands up!" Norris shouted.

Four of the men surrendered, while one brave fool reached for his waist. Tyrone was standing a few feet from the card table and shot him in the head before he could grab his gun.

"Anybody else feeling lucky?" Max asked.

"What's up with that, Mack?" one of them asked. "You set us up!"

"Say one more word, and I'll send you straight to the hereafter!" Max boomed. "All of you stand up!"

The four men stood up with their hands still pointed toward the ceiling, and Tyrone grabbed all their guns, cell phones, and wallets. Norris marched to the kitchen and got the Nike bag while Tyrone tossed the guns and wallets in the bag and motioned his head in the direction of the washroom.

"Somebody in there?" Max asked while still pointing his gun at Tommy G's crew.

"Yeah, Tommy is in there taking a dump," Tyrone replied.

"Come on outta there!" Norris shouted.

"Yeah, pinch that loaf," Tyrone added. "Come on out, Tommy!"

Max crept toward the bathroom door and kicked it open with the hammer of his gun cocked, but the bathroom was empty. The window was open, and the water was still running.

"That coward must have jumped out the window," Tyrone said. "I think the stash is in his room inside the mattress. I'll be right back."

"Lay down on the floor!" Max instructed. "Now!"

The men complied, and Tyrone entered the living room shortly afterward with ten kilos and over ten bundles of hundred-dollar bills in two pillowcases. He then dumped the money and drugs in the gym bag and zipped it up.

"Jackpot," Norris said. "Let's get outta here."

"Damn, that looked like about ten *birds* in that pillowcase," Max said, "and how much loot was that?"

"I counted $130,000," Tyrone answered. "Time to open up shop."

"Y'all don't know who y'all messin' with," one of the men said.

"Didn't I say I'll kill you if you said one more word?!" Max asked tersely.

"Shut the hell up, Joe," Tyrone said. "Since Tommy got away, what are we gonna do with them?"

"Shoot them," Max answered. "It's best to leave no witnesses."

"Oh my God, no!" Joe pleaded. "Don't kill us—word is bond, man—we won't say nothing!"

Norris ignored Joe's plea and shot two of them in the back of the head without hesitation, while Joe and the last guy tried to get up and make a run for the back door. Max let off four shots, hitting Joe in the back and the other guy twice in the chest. Joe was gasping for air and regurgitating blood as the bullet collapsed his left lung, and the other guy lay motionless on the bloody floor. Max stood over Joe momentarily before sending him to his eternal resting place with one more shot.

"I hear sirens!" Tyrone shouted. "Let's bounce!"

"Don't step in the blood," Max urged.

Max grabbed the bag, and the three of them fled out the back door toward the alley. They were at Max's parked car in seconds before they could see flashing lights in the distance of 79th Street. Max peeled off and made a U-turn toward South Shore Drive. He stayed on 79th Street until it merged onto Lake Shore Drive and rode it all the way to 92nd Street. Lake Shore Drive merged onto Ewing Avenue, and Max stayed on Ewing Avenue to Indianapolis Boulevard en route to the Indiana border.

"That was close," Max said. "Someone must have called the cops once gun shots were heard."

"We gotta ditch this car ASAP," Norris urged.

"Why didn't you take 95th Street?" Tyrone asked.

"Because we're three young black males driving around in a bucket at three in the morning," Max answered, "and the block is hot right now. We can't afford to get stopped with drugs and all this cash in the car."

"Where are you headed?" Norris asked.

"I'm gonna look for a spot to ditch this car right here in Hammond," Max answered. "Do me a favor and text Jill, Mack. Tell her to meet us at the gas station on Sibley and State Line Road."

"Okay," Tyrone answered.

"I know of a good spot where we can ditch this ride," Norris said.

"Where?" Max asked.

"Behind that gas station on 137th and Sheffield," Norris answered. "It's a dark road with a railroad track crossing and a trailer park about a half-mile west of there."

"Yeah, I know that road," Max said. "We have to ditch it before daybreak though because I'm gonna set it on fire by the tracks."

"Do you want me to text Jill and tell her to meet us there?" Tyrone asked.

"Yeah, good lookin' out," Max answered.

Tyrone sent Jill the updated text, and Max headed in the direction of the Sheffield Avenue gas station.

"Hopefully, Jill won't take that long to find us," Tyrone said. "I told her to take Sibley East to Hohman Avenue and Hohman to 137th Street."

"She won't have a problem finding it because she's an Uber driver," Max said. "I just hope she wasn't still driving tonight—we're screwed if she ended up in the northwest suburbs or somewhere in the damn boondocks."

"How come you don't Uber?" Norris asked.

"Because I'm a convicted felon," Max answered.

"Oh yeah, that's right," Norris said.

Max reached the gas station and parked the car on the side of it. He checked his watch, and it read three twenty-four. They had less than two hours before daybreak, and Jill texted Tyrone back and said that she was thirty minutes away."

"Jill said she'll be here in thirty minutes," Tyrone said. "So, what now?"

"We sit and wait," Max answered.

10

All the lights were out except for the lamp on the kitchen table, and a wrapped plate of food was sitting on the stove. The clock read a quarter to four as Mitch placed his keys on the kitchen counter. He walked slowly and quietly upstairs to the bedroom to find Sandra sound asleep. He smiled and kissed her on the side of her forehead before taking off his clothes and putting on a t-shirt and sweats.

He went back downstairs and warmed up his food. He continued to daydream about Brea while he ate and fantasized about her warm, sensual kisses he experienced on their impromptu date. He started to feel his nature rise and went back upstairs to finish off what he started with Sandra hours ago. He lifted her nightgown above her perfectly shaped derriere while she lay on her stomach. He almost made the mistake of crying out Brea's name during their late-night festivities after he awakened her but, luckily, caught himself. He held her in his arms until his breathing got back to normal after their quickie, but he was thinking about Brea the entire time.

"Damn, boy, what got into you?" she asked.

"What can I say? I missed you, baby," he said.

"I should send you to the club every night if this is what I'm gonna get afterwards."

"Anything for you—you're the love of my life, sweetheart."

"You mean everything to me, too. Don't ever forget it."

"I promise I won't."

"What time is it?"

"A little after four o'clock. I'm gonna finish eating my food, okay?"

"Alright, baby. I'm going back to sleep."

He went back downstairs to call Brea, but her phone went straight to voicemail.

"I just wanted say I had a great time," he whispered. "I can't wait to see you again. Bye."

He disconnected the call and sat on the living room sofa. He had just made love to his wife physically, but mentally, he was caressing

Brea's unblemished, caramel skin and kissing every inch of her body. He was about to jeopardize his marriage with a woman he barely knew and didn't care.

He had slept with dozens of women while being with Sandra and had always been able to keep his emotions in check—even with Jada. But there was something about Brea—her uniqueness had him spellbound from the very moment their paths crossed at the club.

He grabbed the photo album from the bookcase and started thumbing through pictures of Sandra and him. He tried to convince himself that he could shake off his feelings for Brea, but the true of the matter was there was a powerful magnetic attraction between the two of them that he had never felt with any other woman. His playa ways had caught up with him, and there was nothing he could do about it. His only hope was that Brea treated his now fragile heart with care because he knew deep down that he was playing with fire.

11

Jill arrived at the gas station in a little under a half-hour, and daybreak hadn't come yet, even though the sun was nearing the horizon. She spotted Max's car and parked alongside it before everyone hopped out.

Jill was a very attractive but unladylike young woman. She was the type of girl who would rather shoot craps or play pool than go shopping, or she'd rather sport a pair of Timberlands than wear a pair of stilettos. However, she still had a feminine side in spite of her tomboyish ways. She was Max's Bonnie, and he was her Clyde.

"Hey guys, what's going on?" Jill asked.

"We just robbed these dudes at this card game a little while ago and hit a small jackpot," Max answered, opening the Nike gym bag.

"Damn, you got cash, bricks, and cell phones," Jill said. "How much did y'all get in total?"

"A hundred thirty thousand and ten bricks," Tyrone answered.

"So, we're in the drug game now, baby?" Jill asked Max.

"Nah, I'm gonna have to find somebody to unload these bricks on," Max answered.

"Come on y'all," Norris urged. "We gotta ditch this ride and bounce."

"He's right," Max said. "Let's get outta here."

They left the gas station and drove down the slightly narrow, unlit road and parked at the railroad crossing about three blocks away. Tyrone and Norris hopped inside Jill's truck, and Max went to his trunk and grabbed a white towel that he used when working out at the gym and shoved it halfway down the fuel tank of his car. He then pulled out a lighter from his pocket and lit the towel before hopping inside Jill's truck in the passenger's side seat.

"Let's get the hell outta here!" Max shouted.

Jill sped off, and the four of them watched Max's car become engulfed in flames in the distance from the rear windshield until they couldn't see it anymore. Moments later, they heard a huge explosion as Jill quickly turned left onto Burnham Avenue.

"Man, that was close," Norris said, his heart quickly beating inside his chest.

"Yeah, we're home free," Max said.

"That was a close call, and I can't afford to go back to jail," Tyrone said. "One hundred thirty thousand divided by three is a nice chunk of money. Maybe we should press pause for a minute."

"Nah, we need one more big score, and it's pause for good," Max said."

"Max's right, cuz," Norris said. "We gotta stay focused."

"You mean it, honey?" Jill asked. "One more score and we're done?"

"Yes, baby," Max answered, "one more heist, and we're outta Chicago for good."

They rode the remainder of the ride mostly in silence as Norris and Tyrone fell asleep in the back seat. Max lit a cigarette and sat in deep thought. Jill dropped off Norris first at his apartment off 95th and Michigan, and Tyrone's place was next.

"We'll chop it up at my place at about one o'clock," Max said. "See you later."

"Cool," Norris said. "See you later."

Jill drove off and was at Tyrone's apartment in less than five minutes as he lived about a mile away from Norris. She parked in front of Tyrone's apartment, and the sun had risen in the eastern sky.

"Yo, Max, I need to holla at you about something," Tyrone said. "See you later, Jill."

"Bye, Tyrone," Jill said.

Tyrone got out, and Max said, "I'll be back in a minute."

"Okay, baby," Jill said.

"What up?" Max asked.

"Tommy G knows I set him up, and he's gonna want some payback. Maybe I should settle up and get the hell outta town."

"Well, if you wanna leave, Mack, I won't stop you. Personally, I think Tommy G is a little coward, so I doubt if he comes after you."

"It's Cedric I'm worried about. That's his stash in the bag."

"We hunt down hustlers," Max said. "That's what we do, man. We got a rep now, and most dudes will think twice about running up on us."

"I know, man, but Cedric has an army of soldiers on standby. Going against him is suicide."

"Look, man," Max said, gesturing his hands, "it's not like you to be backing down to anybody. I can't have you watching my back if you're shook, so we can settle up in the morning if you want."

"Yo, that's not what I'm saying," Tyrone said. "You know I got your back, Max, but we need to grow some eyes in the back of our heads from now on."

"I think we'll be fine, Mack. If Cedric wants war, he better come correct because I'll come straight at him."

"I need to get at my cousin Quentin about this new ride he's selling," Tyrone said, changing the subject. "He wants two grand for this '79 Regal he's got."

"So, what's up with him?" Max asked. "Ain't he the man out west?"

"Yeah, Quentin's got the dope game sewed up out there, and he's into a lot of other stuff, too," Tyrone answered. "As a matter of fact, he says he working on something big—real big."

"Did he say what it is?"

"It's this new club called uh—*Club*—uh—*Club Ecstasy*. They sometimes make three, maybe four hundred thousand on some nights. He said he likes the way we handle business and wants to do the job with us."

"Straight? Yo, let's set something up with him. If this club has as much loot as you say it does, this is my last score. We hit 'em hard, and it's *adios*, my brother."

"What? Where would you go?"

"I don't know yet, but I'm definitely getting the hell outta Chicago. There's nothing keeping me here."

"I hear you, Max, but what are we gonna do about flippin' these *birds*? If you leave, I can't move them without you. Maybe we should find somebody to take 'em off our hands."

"You think Quentin will want to take 'em off our hands?"

"Maybe, I don't know. He doesn't really mess with coke. Heroin is what he moves, and he moves a ton of it."

"Well, maybe we should hold on to it until we pull off this last job. You know, we can all leave town together—you, me, and Norris, bruh."

"I'm with you, dawg."

12

It was Friday—almost a week later—and Mitch still hadn't heard from Brea. He was sitting at his desk at work trying to focus but couldn't. I think I still got some cool points, he thought. She probably thought I was trying to run game when I said I was already in love with her. She can't know how deeply I've fallen for her—she will destroy me without giving it a second thought. I've done some pretty nasty things to a lot of women, and now I know how they must have felt.

I have to chill—I left her two messages but won't leave a third one. She has my numbers, so if she really wants to get with me, she's gonna have to be the one to call. I refuse to sweat her, and the quickest way to turn a girl off is to hound her.

He knew that she knew she was holding all the cards because he played his hand too soon, and he was mad at himself for allowing his feelings to cloud his better judgment. Everything was great at home, and he wanted to keep it that way. He didn't have the time or the patience to chase Brea, no matter how fine she was. He also needed to find a way to let Jada down easy because he came to the conclusion that what he did to her was selfish, and he was feeling guilty about leading her on. He knew she deserved better than what he was able to give her.

He also knew that women like Brea made it their business to break and shake guys whose game was weak, and he realized he had fallen into that category as far as she was concerned. He knew he wasn't all that special to her at that point and didn't want to be just another simp in her orbit, and he needed to snap out of his trance and somehow turn the tables on her. His male ego was also shattered—it didn't matter that he had dozens of notches under his belt because all he could see was she didn't return the love he felt for her.

His office phone rang incessantly all day because of a very important report he had due for an important client. The correct financial analysis of this client's company could lead to a possible partnership for him at the firm, but he couldn't stop thinking about Brea. He did manage to finish the report before the five o'clock deadline and was relieved, but he felt like he didn't do his best work.

His phone rang again, and he thought about not answering it. However, he saw that it was Jada's number, so he picked up on the third ring.

"Hello," he said.

"Hi, baby," Jada said. "I was wondering if you could swing by my job when you get off work."

"Sure, Jada, that shouldn't be a problem."

"Good, because I have something I need to share with you."

"What is it?"

"Not now, Mitch. I'll tell you when you get here—I'll take my break when you call."

"Okay, see you later."

He hung up the phone and pondered what Jada could possibly want. He thought about the possibility that she might want to break up with him because he had been neglecting her. He also thought it might be possible that she was pregnant. Whatever it was, curiosity caused him to be suddenly antsy.

It was a quarter to six, and he decided to call it a day. He said goodnight to his assistant Connie and hastened to the parking lot. He wanted to find a way to tell Jada the truth and let the chips fall where they may, but he decided to hear her out first and take it from there.

His job wasn't too far from hers, so he parked by a meter half a block from her building when he got there. He then called her desk and told her he was parked downstairs. He stood outside his car to smoke a cigarette so that she could see him, and she came down to greet him not long afterwards.

"Hi, baby," she said, hugging him and kissing him on the cheek. "Do you have somewhere to be?"

"Yeah, I was gonna swing by the club later on to help Wes," he answered.

"Let's take a drive somewhere—anywhere."

"Okay, but what's this about?"

"I'll tell you once we get out of here."

They drove off in the direction of the near north side down Orleans Street in an attempt to avoid rush hour traffic. He asked her if she wanted something to eat. She shook her head no and said, "Did you talk to your wife about getting a divorce?"

"Uh, no, babe," he answered with nervousness in his voice. "It's been so hectic at work and at the club. I haven't had a chance to sit down with her. You know, the timing just hasn't been right."

"The timing hasn't been right for a year now, Mitch, but that's not even why I have you driving me around."

"What is it then, baby? Spit it out."

"I've been offered a job to write for the New York Post, and I accepted the offer. It's a once-in-a-lifetime opportunity, and you just proved to me that there's nothing really keeping me here."

"So you're just gonna take the job without talking to me first? That's messed up, Jada."

"No, what's messed up is you made promises to me that you knew you couldn't keep. I'm tired of putting my life on hold for you."

"I'm sorry, Jada. You're right. I can't give you the commitment you deserve, and I feel terrible about it. I hope you can forgive me for letting you down."

"No need for apologies, Mitch. I went in with both eyes open. I called you so that we could say goodbye to each other. I'm leaving at the beginning of next month now that I'm officially done with grad school."

"Wow, I don't know what to say—will we ever see each other again?"

"I don't know—nobody knows what the future holds."

"Can we at least keep in touch?"

"Sure, maybe when I get settled in, I'll call you. I will always love you, Mitch. You were my first."

"I will always love you, too."

They drove around for another fifteen minutes or so before he dropped her back off at work. She kissed him on the lips before getting out of his car and turned around one last time to wave before entering the building, and the finality of the situation made him shed a tear. She gut-punched him by telling him that she was moving to New York, and enormous feelings of guilt and regret overwhelmed him momentarily.

He drove off and headed in the direction of the club once he regained his composure. He wiped away another tear and made a vow to himself to get his personal life together. Even though Sandra was the love of his life, Jada was his first love, and the void of her absence was going to be hard to fill.

13

Tyrone had taken Max to meet his cousin Quentin about a possible score that could potentially yield enough money for all of them to leave Chicago for good. Max had expressed a desire to leave the game and open a carwash or barbershop somewhere. He dreamt of owning his own business, even when he was an undergrad student at Texas Southern. He had talked about it quite often when he was Mitch's roommate. Mitch made his dreams come true while Max settled for being a thief and killer. He knew he was meant to do so much more than hunt down drug dealers.

They arrived at Quentin's corner store in K-Town on the west side and went to the back. The clerk led them to the basement of the store where Quentin was. He had heroin wrapped in plastic bags spread across a table and was counting money with a bill counter machine.

"What's up, Big Ty," Quentin said. "Is this Max?"

"Yeah, cuz," Tyrone answered. "This is the man I've been telling you about."

"Good to finally meet you," Quentin said, extending his hand toward Max. "I've been hearing good things about you from Ty and my little brother, boss. I love the way y'all handle business."

"It's all good, Quentin," Max said. "I'm just livin', man."

"You're doing more than livin', bro," Quentin said, "and that's the main reason why I need you and your crew to help me pull off this job. This new club that opened up a year or so ago is raking in mad loot every week, and I think it's time we tax them."

"I'm definitely in, Quentin," Max said. "How much do you think we can get?"

"If we hit 'um tomorrow, there should be over a million dollars in there," Quentin answered. "Brink's comes three times a week—early Tuesday, early Thursday, and early Sunday. We will split the loot four ways—you, me, Ty and Norris."

"That sounds like a great plan, but how are we gonna bring heat in the club?" Max asked. "I'm sure a club that size checks people at the door."

"I got that covered, homeboy," Quentin answered. "My girl Bria strips there every Thursday. She smuggled the guns inside already...I got her to duct tape four Glocks under the stalls in the men's bathroom when no one was looking."

"Damn, man, that was genius," Tyrone added. "Nobody will suspect a thing."

"Yeah, and we can hit 'um tomorrow at midnight," Quentin said. "They count the money around that time, and I have masks that we can use once we get the guns from the bathroom."

"How many bouncers do we have to take out before we get to the loot?" Max asked.

"Bria said there are usually five or six of 'um throughout the club," Quentin answered. "Two of 'um stand by the door when they are counting the money."

"Let's do it," Max said.

"Count me in, too," Tyrone added. "Norris is also down for whatever."

"Good then, gents," Quentin said. "It's settled. We waste no time droppin' these fools. In and out."

"No doubt," Max said, giving Quentin some dap.

"We're out, Q," Tyrone said.

"Let's meet up at about seven tomorrow to go over the logistics one more time," Quentin said.

Both men nodded and walked back upstairs, and the clerk unlocked the door once he heard their footsteps. Tyrone bought two forty ounces of Colt 45, and they left.

"You really think we can pull this off?" Tyrone asked, taking a swig of his beer. "A million dollars is a lot of dough."

"It'll be like taking candy from a baby, Mack," Max answered. "They'll never see us coming. Two hundred fifty thousand a piece is definitely worth the risk."

"No doubt about it, homeboy," Tyrone said. "Let's get this money."

14

Mitch was in the office of the club, where the safe was and where he did the books. Wesley handled most of the daily operations of the club, like making sure the bar was fully stocked, booking the DJ's, and helping the staff serve the patrons who frequented their spot.

Mitch was looking over some invoices, while reminiscing about his first encounter with Jada after graduating from college. He had just purchased his home in Lynwood with Sandra, and he had needed to go to Target to pick up some accessories for the house.

It was almost ten o'clock at night—about eighteen minutes before closing—and before entering the store, he was stopped in his tracks by this drop-dead gorgeous young woman in a tight-fitting tan blouse and matching miniskirt with six-inch stilettos. Her silky hair draped down her shoulders, and her Gucci pumps accentuated her shapely legs. He didn't really focus on her face because he was totally spellbound by her curvaceous frame and walked right past her. She had walked that fine line of sexy versus sleazy but had pulled it off nicely.

"Mitch, is that you?" Jada asked.

"Jada?" he asked. "Damn, I'm sorry. I didn't recognize you. You look amazing."

"Thank you, so do you. It's been ages since we've seen each other."

"I know, right? I just bought a house out here with my wife, and we're just settling in."

"Wow, congratulations, Mitch. I just bought a house out here, too, and I'm about to start graduate school."

"That's great, Jada. I see both of us are doing big things. Your husband is a lucky man."

"What makes you think I'm married?"

"A woman as fine as you can't possibly be single."

"Well, I am, Mitch. I can't seem to find the right guy, and besides, I'm too busy with work and school."

"Oh yeah, what do you do?"

"I'm a shift manager at a check processing company, and I've been there since I finished undergrad."

"Banking, huh? I thought you majored in journalism."

"I did, but banking pays the bills. I'm going to grad school, so I can have the proper credentials to be a journalist."

"I hear you, Jada. I was lucky—I found a job as a financial analyst when I interned my junior and senior year, and they hired me permanently once I graduated."

"That's wonderful. Well, it was nice seeing you again. Take care."

"Wait," he said, gently grabbing her arm.

"Yes, what is it?" she asked with a seductive smile.

"Can I have your number? Maybe we could have lunch sometime."

"What about your wife? I'm sure she wouldn't appreciate you trying to reconnect with an old flame."

"It's just lunch. What's the harm in that?"

"Okay, just lunch."

And the rest was history. They had carried on an affair for almost two years before it ended earlier that day. He didn't think breaking up with her would be very hard until it happened. It was more the fact that she beat him to the punch, but he also knew deep down inside that the relationship had run its course. He would miss her but splitting up was the best thing for both of them.

Moments later, Wesley walked in the office. He was sipping on a drink and had a ridiculous grin on his face.

"What are you smiling about?" Mitch asked. "You should see yourself in the mirror."

"Damn, man, what's got your panties in a bunch?" Wesley asked. "Why can't a brutha just be happy? Man, business is great, cuz."

"I know—sorry to piss on your parade. Jada and I just ended things between us tonight."

"Yeah? Sorry to hear that, man. I really liked her—she's good peoples."

"Yeah, I'm gonna miss her, but it's for the best."

Wesley paused and asked, "Who was that honey you left with the other night? She was top notch."

"Nobody, man," Mitch said frowning. "Messing around with her was a colossal waste of my damn time."

"Touchy, touchy. I think you need a drink."

"I most certainly do. Give me a Hennessy straight with a little ice if you don't mind."

"No problem, coming right up."

Wesley poured a glass of Hennessy on the rocks and handed Mitch his glass before taking a sip of his own.

"You know what your problem is, Mitch?"

"No, what is it, Dr. Freud?"

"You don't know how to just hit it and quit it."

"Hit it and quit it? What-the-hell are you talking about?"

"You break the rules by getting too involved with women who are just supposed to be side pieces. You should have just slept with Jada and moved on. Don't get me wrong; she's a good woman, but you can't give her what she wants, so why entertain it?"

"I don't know. I guess I'm not cut out for the game anymore now that I'm older and more settled."

"You get too damn emotional—when I was out there—I never let my feelings get the best of me because I didn't stay around long enough for them to sink in."

"Well, I'm done, Wes. From now on, it's just me and Sandra."

"I'll drink to that."

They tapped glasses and Mitch said, "Enough about me. How are Marsol and little Wesley doing?"

"They're good, cuz. Thanks for asking. We're trying to have another, you know, give little Wesley a playmate."

"That's great, man. Maybe Sandra and I will start a family soon."

"What's the problem? You two ain't getting no younger."

"She wants to establish her career first, but the truth of the matter is that I don't think she wants kids. It's been five years, and she still doesn't know what she wants to do. She's about to start school again."

"What do you want, Mitch?"

"I wanted three or four kids, but I'm not so sure that kids are in our future. I don't pressure her, but I'm starting to get impatient."

"I hate to say this, but you two have never really been on the same page. I love Sandra, but Jada was a better fit for you in my opinion."

"Thanks, man, now I'm even more confused than I was a couple of hours ago."

"Keep drinking this Hennessy, and you won't give a damn about either one of them—at least for the night, anyway."

"Great advice, cuz," Mitch said sarcastically, "just great."

"See you later, man. You really need to lighten up."

"Whatever, man."

Mitch gulped the last of his drink and poured another one. Wesley returned to the main floor to mingle and manage the staff. Mitch had decided to call it quits with the paperwork and join Wesley on the floor. *Club Ecstasy* was a bi-level club that could house up to 2,000 people comfortably and about 2,500-3,000 people elbow to elbow on their busiest nights. They didn't use any fancy, textbook marketing schemes to attract people—just good old-fashioned word-of-mouth advertising and hot girls made the club popular.

Mitch made his way to the main level and observed the crowd starting to pick up. He found a spot at the end of the bar and stood there briefly. The dance floor was packed as Future's "Commas" blared through the speakers.

"You wanna dance, handsome?" a young lady asked.

"No thanks, baby," Mitch replied. "I'll take a rain check, okay?"

"Sure, I'll hold you to that," she answered.

The young lady walked away, and Mitch continued to scan the club. That was when he spotted Brea hugged up with another guy at one of the booths alongside the wall. A cold chill came over him that was stronger than butterflies but not quite as strong as the feeling of being completely heartbroken. It felt like seeing his first crush kiss another boy instead of him. He stared in disbelief and wondered how she'd have the gall to show up in his club with someone else.

He wanted to walk up to them and say, "You and friend, get the hell out of my club, ho!"

However, what he ended up saying was, "Hello, Brea, aren't you going to introduce me to your friend?"

"Hi, Mitch, this is Calvin," she answered.

Mitch extended his hand and said, "Nice to meet you, Calvin. Any friend of Brea's is a friend of mine. What are you all drinking?"

"Bacardi and Coke," Calvin answered.

"You know I like my drinks straight," Brea added. "Give me a shot of tequila."

Mitch flagged down one of the barmaids and said, "Give them as many drinks as they want on the house. Enjoy the club, Calvin."

"Thanks, Mitch," he said. "That's mighty nice of you."

"Don't mention it," Mitch said. "Take care, Brea."

"Bye, Mitch," she said with a perplexed grin on her face.

Mitch walked away with a little bit of satisfaction. I know she expected me to go off, he thought. I'll kill her with kindness—if I can't get with her, I can at least get her and her friends to spend money at my club. He tried to convince himself that it was just business from that point on, nothing personal.

He went back upstairs to finish working. He was always a bit of a workaholic—an overachiever, who pulled himself up by his bootstraps and became a millionaire before thirty. He continued to work until closing, and he wanted to get a cup of coffee to perk up before his long drive home. He talked to Sandra around seven and knew she'd probably be asleep by the time he got there. He planned on giving her an encore performance from last week the moment he stepped in the front door.

He went downstairs and said his goodbyes to Wesley and each one of his staff members. He valued each employee he had and rarely passed up an opportunity to let each one of them know it.

He briskly walked toward his car and noticed Brea staggering toward the corner. She appeared to be headed in the direction of Harlem Avenue—possibly to flag down a cab or catch an Uber, so he quickly tried to get her attention before she reached the end of the block.

"Brea!" he shouted. "Come on, I'll give you a ride!"

"Yeah, I just bet you wanna give me a ride all right!" she shouted back. "Leave me alone!"

"Quit playing, Brea," he said. "Come on. Get in—I'll save you from having to pay for a cab or an Uber."

Brea stumbled before reaching for the door and plopped inside. She mumbled something unintelligible and put her head in her lap.

"Are you okay?" Mitch asked.

"I-feel-like-crap," she slurred.

"Where do you live, Brea?"

"Dearborn Park," she mumbled. "Do you know where it is? It's an exclusive community."

"Yes, I know where it is. Looks like you had a little too much to drink—I guess I'm somewhat responsible for that, and I apologize. Where's your date—what's his name—uh, Calvin, right?"

"We had a fight, and he left me."

"I'm sorry about that, Brea. I really am."

"You're such a sweet guy, Mitch. All Calvin wanted to do was sleep with me—but not you, Mitch—you really do care about me. All guys ever want to do is have sex! Ever since I was twelve—my uncle tried to rape me, and so did my ninth grade algebra teacher. As soon as I told Calvin he wasn't getting any tonight, he freakin' left me!"

"Calm down, Brea. I'm going to get you home safely—I promise. Don't worry, okay?"

"Thank you, Mitch. You're so nice to me—even when I wasn't so nice to you. I'm very sorry—I just thought you were like all the others. I wanted to make you chase me for it—to see how bad you wanted it."

Mitch reached inside the compartment in the middle of the front seats and grabbed a bottle of Tylenol. He handed her the bottle and adjusted the volume of his radio.

"You're gonna have to take them dry," he said. "I can stop at a gas station for something to drink if you want."

"No, thank you. I'm cool," she said.

They drove in silence for the remainder of the ride, and she fell asleep with her head on his shoulder. He lightly caressed her hair for a brief moment while focusing on the road. Once he was a couple of blocks from her place, he gently tapped her on the shoulder to wake her up.

"We're here," he said. "How do I get in?"

"Turn left at the stop light," she said as she yawned, "and then go to the end of the block and turn right."

He put the car in park and turned to face her.

"I really appreciate what you did for me," she said, leaning over to kiss him on the cheek. "Sorry about my meltdown."

"No apology is necessary," he said. "Do you need me to walk you to your door?"

"No, I can take it from here. Thanks."

"Okay. Take care, Brea."

"Goodbye, Mitch."

She grabbed her purse off the floor and got out, and he watched her go in before driving off. He studied the way her stretch-denim jeans hugged her hips, thighs, and rear end, and he marveled at the way her tube top covered her ample bosom and exposed her midriff without a roll or stretch mark on her back or stomach. She was a vision of perfection—even when she was at one of the lowest moments of her life.

"She has way too much baggage," he said to himself. "I can't risk what I've built with Sandra, no matter how I feel about her."

He cranked up his music as he entered the expressway. He then cruised in the express lane and didn't give Brea another thought for the rest of the night.

15

"Let's go over the plan more time," Quentin said.

"Damn, I think we got it, Q," Tyrone said tersely. "We went over this three times already."

"It's cool, Mack," Max interjected. "It's like running drills on the basketball court. We have to practice, so there are no mistakes. One false move, and we're all dead."

"Listen to your boy, cuz," Quentin said. "You straight, Norris?"

"Cool as a fan, bro," Norris answered.

"I have one suggestion, fellas," Max said, looking in Quentin's direction. "I think we need a getaway driver. We're not gonna have time to run to the car once we air out this joint."

"He's right, Q," Tyrone said. "We need a fifth person."

"What about the chick who put the guns in the men's bathroom, big bro?" Norris asked. "We're just gonna have to split the loot five ways."

"Okay, I'll put her on, but don't worry about splitting the score five ways," Quentin answered. "Everybody's cut will still be the same, and I'll pay her outta my cut."

"Cool, it's settled then," Max said.

Quentin gave them the layout of the club one last time—one bouncer at the front door, one at the back door, and the remaining four circulating throughout the entire club. Two are stationed at the office door every time money is being counted, and the back door is locked from the outside but unlocked on the inside when no one is manning it. The fire code doesn't allow the door to be chained with a padlock.

The plan was to go inside the men's room one at a time in thirty-second intervals and enter one of the four stalls one by one. Once the fourth stall was available, the last guy would shut the door and tap it three times once he unfastened the gun from underneath the toilet. They would put on their masks and head toward the money room after the signal was made. Anyone who approached them would be shot on sight. Each guy would have a twenty-gallon Hefty bag in his pocket to load the cash. They would only have three to five minutes at the most to pull off the job.

"Once we get the money, we'll slip out the back door," Quentin instructed. "If someone's watching the door, shoot him."

"Tell me something. Why are there only four stalls in a club this size?" Tyrone asked.

"Good question," Quentin answered. "I really don't know."

"Do they serve food in there?" Max asked.

"Nah, just drinks," Quentin answered.

"How many urinals does the bathroom have?" Max asked.

"Eight, maybe ten," Quentin answered. "Why?"

"My guess would be that the owner probably doesn't want nobody taking dumps in his club," Max answered, "and that's why there are only four stalls."

"Damn, you're probably right about that," Quentin said. "I never would've given it a second thought."

"So, is everybody ready?" Max asked.

Everyone nodded, and Quentin said, "Alright, let's head on over to the club, and I'll have Bria meet us there."

16

Brea had called Mitch because she was stranded on Lake Shore Drive with a flat tire. He left Wesley to run the shop alone on one of their busiest nights ever. He explained to him what was going on and told him if anybody asked where he was, he was going to the currency exchange to get some singles for the cash registers. He wanted to cover his tracks in case Sandra called the club.

His intentions were to fix her flat and double back to the club to help Wesley count the money for the Brink's pickup at six o'clock in the morning. He exited the Dan Ryan Expressway at Thirty-Ninth Street and headed toward the lakefront. He spotted Brea's shiny, jet-black Mustang sitting on the right-hand shoulder of the northbound side of the Drive. It was a little after dusk, so he would have to change her tire in the dark.

He parked behind her car and turned on his hazard lights, and when she stepped out of her car, she had on a black miniskirt that barely covered her crotch. He tried to focus on the problem at hand, which was getting her tire off and putting the spare on faster than a crew at NASCAR, but he practically undressed her with his eyes instead. He looked for some sort of panty line or imprint of a thong but couldn't find one.

"Thanks for coming, Mitch," Brea said. "I had no one else to call."

"You sounded pretty urgent over the phone, Brea," Mitch said. "I couldn't just leave you hanging."

"Well, I really appreciate this."

"No problem. Let me get to it because I have to head back to the club."

Mitch popped the trunk and saw that she had a regular tire instead of the standard, hold-me-over donut tire. She also had a real jack and crowbar instead of the factory issued set. He then observed that her flat was the front tire on the right side.

"This makes my job a whole lot easier," he said. "Thank you."

"I didn't like that cheap spare and jack that came with the car," she said. "I don't know how it happened—I probably ran over a nail or something."

"I'm just glad you weren't hurt."

"You're so sweet, Mitch. Once again, I'm really sorry about the way I behaved before. You didn't deserve that."

"I don't know about all that, Brea. I did come on a little strong, though."

"It's still no excuse. Can we just start over?"

"Yes, but as friends only," he said, wiping some sweat from his forehead. "Look, like I said before, you don't owe me any apologies or explanations. I'm a married man, and you're a beautiful, single lady having fun."

"I know you're a married man, Mitch," she said with an attitude. "We established the rules in the very beginning."

"Rules? There are no rules. I have a good woman, who loves me and only me, so I need to focus on that."

"It's a beautiful thing to have someone love you, but how do you really feel about her? I thought we had something going on—you can't deny the chemistry between us even if you wanted to."

"You're right. I'm very attracted to you, but I don't have the time to compete with some other guy for your attention."

"You mean Calvin? He doesn't mean anything to me—he was supposed to be helping me get a record deal; that's all."

"It's cool, sweetheart. I really need to concentrate on getting my marriage back on track, anyway. I guess I should thank you for helping me realize what's really important."

He tightened the last bolt on the tire about fifteen minutes later and said, "Well, you're set—I gotta get back to the club. Good luck with your demo and don't hesitate call me if you ever need anything else, okay?"

"Don't go," she said, gazing in his eyes. "I really want to show you my appreciation for being such a gentleman. Your cousin can do without you for a couple of hours."

"What did you have in mind?"

"I'm a great cook, so let me whip something up for you. You know that my place isn't that far from here, so come on. It'll be great."

"Alright then, you lead the way."

He followed her back to her place, and once they were inside, she turned on some soft jazz to set the mood before getting dinner started. He went the bathroom to clean himself up a bit, and she changed into something more comfortable.

He sat down on her living room sofa after washing his hands and face. He observed the various paintings throughout her condo and the canvas that was incomplete. She came out of her bedroom a few minutes later with a tight-fitting t-shirt that displayed her protruding nipples, skin-tight blue jeans shorts and flip-flops.

"You're a regular Renaissance woman, huh?" he asked. "Singing and painting, and you can cook."

"I don't wanna toot my own horn," she answered, "but yes, I'm good at all of those things."

"You're artist in every sense of the word. Do you display your work anywhere?"

"Yeah, I have a couple of paintings at the Art Institute, but nothing more than that. I don't do it for the money."

"Well, you should...these are really good."

"Thank you. So, do you want anything in particular to eat? I have chicken, steak, and pork chops, and I have some fresh greens in the fridge."

"Damn, you throw down like that? I'll let you decide."

"How about fried chicken and greens? I'll even throw in some fresh mashed potatoes if you like."

"That sounds great. Do you need me to do anything?"

"No, baby, just sit back and relax. I have some beer in the fridge, too. Do you like Heineken?"

"Yes, I do."

"Coming right up."

She brought him the beer and went back to the kitchen to finish preparing their meal. He took a gulp of his beer and turned on the television. A rerun episode of *Power* was on, so he tuned into that, instead of the jazz on the radio. Fifteen minutes into the show, his phone rang.

"Hello," he said.

"Yo, cuz, when are you coming back?" Wesley asked.

"Hey, Wes, I don't know yet. Can you believe she's cooking me dinner?"

"Yeah? Well, I guess you're gonna be tied up for a while. We got a boatload of cash to count for Brink's, so just get back as soon as you can."

"Alright, Wes, see you in a bit."

He disconnected the call and continued to watch *Power*. He noticed there weren't any pictures of friends or family throughout her place, but at that moment, he remembered her telling him that her parents were deceased. He thought the memory of them was probably too painful for her.

He started flicking through channels with the remote once the episode ended and found the news. He caught the beginning, and the first topic was the five murders on the southeast side last weekend. They named Tommy Glenn as a person of interest in the case.

"Did you hear about those murders near that club last weekend?" he asked.

"Huh?" she asked.

"The murders...did you hear about those five guys who were shot to death last weekend?"

"Yeah, I did hear about that. This world is getting crazier by the day."

"I know, and I bet it had to be over drugs. Hey, I know that guy that they're talking about."

"Come in the kitchen and keep me company. The food will be ready soon."

"Where did you learn how to cook?" he asked, sitting down at the kitchen table.

"My grandmother taught me everything I know. She died right before my parents did."

"Do you have any family left?"

"I have a twin sister...her name is Bria. We moved here together, and she stays in Oak Park."

"Brea and Bria—you two are close, huh?"

"Yeah, we're like you and your cousin Wesley."

"Are you all identical or fraternal twins?"

"We're fraternal twins—she's just a lighter version of me."

"I see. So, who's the oldest?"

"I am by twelve minutes."

He paused and asked, "How does Chicago compare to New York?"

"I like Chicago a lot, but there's no place like home," she answered. "Things close here after a certain time, but New York never shuts down."

"I've never been there, so I'll have to put it on my things-to-do list."

"I think you'll love it. Maybe we can do it together one day."

"Maybe we will."

"So, how did you get into the nightclub business?" she asked, changing the subject.

"Wes and I put up the money to open the club, and we were fortunate that it took off the way it did. We're 50/50 partners."

"Where did you come up with that kind of money, if you don't mind me asking?"

"Nah, I don't mind—that's a fair question. I make good money at the firm but not enough to invest in a business alone. I got some stock tips that really paid off for me—so much so that I was able to invest in the club with Wes with no issues."

"Where did Wesley get his share of the money?"

"Well, let's just say that Wes was in the catering business if you know what I mean."

"Indeed, I do, Mitch."

She paused briefly and said, "I want to open my own art gallery soon after I get a record deal."

"I'm sure that your dreams will come true," he said.

"Well, the food is just about ready. Do you want another beer or something else to drink?"

"A beer is fine, and the food smells good. I can't wait to try it."

She fixed their plates, they ate, and they continued to talk about their pasts until they were both stuffed. They popped down on her living room sofa together, and she snuggled with him. He put his arm around her while she scrolled channels trying to find something for them to watch.

"Dinner was unbelievable," he said. "I ate so much I can barely move. Thank you so much."

"You're very welcome."

She placed the remote on the table and sat on his lap facing him with her legs folded. She kissed him lightly on his lips and smiled at him.

"You are so sexy to me, Mitch," she said. "I just wanted you to know that. No more games, okay?"

"What happened to your five-date rule?"

"Just shut up and kiss me."

He pulled her close and kissed her passionately. He felt his nature rise once he gripped her soft and sexy rear end. She then lifted her shirt above her head and tossed it on the floor. He marveled at her ample bosom and flawless skin as he caressed every inch of her body.

"That feels so good, baby," she said.

"You look so damn beautiful," he said. "I want to kiss you from head to toe."

"Let's take this to the bedroom, baby," she said.

They completely disrobed themselves and entered her seductive lair. They started kissing passionately once again and fell onto the bed—and after thoroughly satisfying each other, they lay euphorically in the afterglow of their intense lovemaking session in each other's arms.

"Damn, girl, what the hell did you just do to me?" he asked.

"Make sweet love to you, baby," she answered. "I can give you this every night if you want me to."

"You're making this very hard, Brea."

"That's my intention, and if you stick with me, I'm gonna make sure you don't have anything left to give your wife. Sooner or later, you will have to make a decision between us."

"It's a nice problem to have, but you're right about one thing. I won't have anything left once I get home tonight because you wore me out."

"You wore me out, too, baby," she said, winking at him.

She continued to smile at him and said, "I noticed you usually don't come to the club until Thursday or Friday, so your wife can have you Monday through Wednesday. However, you're mine for the rest of the week."

"So, you're been checking me out, huh? Wow, I don't know what to say...I'm very flattered."

"Yes, I've been coming to your club every week for the last month, hoping to see you again. What took you so long to notice me?"

"I really don't know because you're pretty hard to miss. Just don't be giving your candy away to strangers when I'm not there, Brea."

"You really think you're funny, don't you? I don't even get down like that."

"I'm just saying I don't think I can handle that."

"Don't worry, Mitch. Once I commit to someone, I'm a one-man woman. That gold-digger impression I gave you when we first met isn't who I really am, either. As you can clearly see, I'm very catering to my man, and I love very hard."

"I must say I'm very impressed with you, Brea, and I've never met anyone like you."

"I know you haven't met anyone like me because I'm one of a kind."

"Yes, you are," Mitch said as he rose from the bed.

"And where do you think you're going?" she said, raising an eyebrow.

"Whoa—down, girl. I'm just going to the bathroom to take a leak. You can watch if you like."

"I was just making sure—you do owe me one more round, baby."

"I think I can do that."

17

Norris sat in the middle of the bar and noticed a pretty girl at the end of it smiling at him. He turned around to see if she was looking at someone else, and there were only women seated to the left of him. He turned back around, and her smile widened as she shook her head at him. The wannabe playa smiled back at her and rose from his seat with drink in hand and approached her.

She was checking him out, but not for the reason he thought she was. She had been sipping on the same glass of Coke for the last twenty minutes, and her intention was to find the first available guy in the club to buy her next drink. Cognac and Coke was her drink of choice for the next round, and Norris was the unknowing participant in her scheme.

"Hey, beautiful, I'm Norris," he said.

"Nice to meet you, Norris," she said. "I'm Kia."

"Nice to meet you, too. What are you drinking?"

"Hennessy and Coke would be nice."

"I got you. So, you come here often?"

"Nah, it's just my second time. It was jumpin' the first night I was here, so figured I'd check it out this weekend."

"Well, I'm glad you did...your pretty smile definitely made my night."

"Thank you, Norris. So, what do you do for a living?"

"Damn, you get right to it, don't you?"

"I like to know upfront whether I'm wasting my time."

"A woman who knows what she wants...I like that. Well, I'm a licensed carpenter by trade. I buy distressed properties, I rehab them, and I sell them for a profit. If you or somebody you know needs work done, here's my card."

Norris was in fact a licensed carpenter, but he embellished the part about flipping properties. He used that line to pick up women every chance he got.

She looked over the card and said, "Wow that's very impressive, Mr. Norris Adams. So, what do you do for fun?"

"Fun is whatever you think fun is, sweetheart. Maybe you could show me what that is one day soon."

"I like your style, handsome. Do you wanna dance?"

"Sure, baby, lead the way."

Kia took Norris's hand and led him to the crowded dance floor, and Quentin and another girl walked off the dance floor and headed toward the bar. Quentin had been eyeing this girl since he stepped inside the club—a master manipulator, who stalked his prey and didn't waste any time going in for the kill. There were two vacant seats at the far end of the bar nearest the entrance. They sat down, and Quentin waved his hand to get the bartender's attention.

"Whatcha drinkin', pretty lady?" he asked her.

"I'll have a strawberry daiquiri if you don't mind," she answered.

"My name is Quentin by the way."

"I'm Renee...nice to meet you."

"You're not from around here, are you?" he said.

"No, I'm not," she answered. "How can you tell?"

"Your accent gave you away. Boston or New York?"

"I'm from Newark actually. I'm here visiting my sister."

"Well, in that case, welcome to Chicago," he said, gulping down one of his three shots.

"Thank you, Quentin," she said, taking a sip of her daiquiri. "You come here often?"

"Not often, but I've been here a few times since it opened."

"This is really a nice club. I just turned twenty-one, and this is only the second club I've ever been to."

"Are you serious? You must be a college student, huh?"

"Yes, I am. I'm going to be a senior at St. Johns University."

"Oh yeah, what's your major?"

"Accounting."

"Yeah? I'm gonna need somebody to manage my money for me. When you graduate, I can be your first client."

"Wow, I don't know what to say. I'm flattered, but I have to pass my CPA exam before I become certified."

"I'm sure that won't be a problem for a smart girl like you."

She blushed and said, "So, what is your profession?"

"I have five buildings that I own and manage, and I own a small grocery store. Does that sound like something you can handle?"

"Yes, I think I can handle that," she smiled.

"Good. Wanna another drink?"

"Sure."

Tyrone was on the other end of the club on the wall sipping on his Crown Royal on the rocks. He wasn't really feeling the spot at all—he would've been happy just going to a strip club first and showing up at *Club Ecstasy* fifteen minutes before game time. He was a soldier, who played his position and played it well. The only thing he did enjoy about the club was the DJ throwing down on the turntables.

"Buy me a drink, handsome," a young lady said.

"Sorry, but I'm all tapped out, sexy," Tyrone said, "but you can buy me one."

"Excuse me?" she asked sarcastically.

"You heard me—I said you can buy me one."

"You must be crazy, boy."

"Get outta my face, you stuck-up trick!"

"Go to hell!"

Max pretty much felt the same way Tyrone did, but he was much better at hiding it. He was also the strong and silent type, who approached everyday life like a game of chess. He had already played out ten probable outcomes in his head before they even arrived at the club. He was standing a few feet away from Tyrone with a half-finished Miller Draft in his right hand. He also cleaned himself up rather nicely from his usual t-shirt, Timberlands, and faded jeans.

"Compliments of the young lady sitting at the table," the barmaid said, handing him another beer and pointing in a beautiful young lady's direction.

"Thank you," Max said, looking in the woman's direction and lifting his second bottle of Miller Draft in the air to acknowledge her.

He gulped the rest of his first beer and walked over to her table.

He placed the empty bottle on the vacant table in front of her and said, "Thank you for the drink, gorgeous. You didn't have to do that."

"I know I didn't have to do that," she said, "but I wanted to do it. My name is Tammy."

"Gary," he said, shaking her hand.

"So, Gary, what's a girl gotta do to be down with you, huh?"

"I'm a simple guy, Tammy. It doesn't take much to please me."

"That's good to know. Look, what do you say we get outta here and go somewhere?"

"Your offer sounds very tempting, but I'mma have to pass, beautiful. I'm waiting for someone to meet me, and she should be here soon."

"Lucky girl."

"I feel like I'm the lucky one. Well, thanks again for the drink."

"You're welcome, baby. I'll see you around."

Max looked up at the VIP room and the office a few feet away from it on the second floor and saw two of the bouncers standing around as if they were guarding the area. The office door was closed with the light on, so Max gave Tyrone the signal, which was to light a Black & Mild cigar and take a puff of it. Max didn't smoke Black & Mild, so Tyrone, on cue, headed toward the end of the bar and asked the beautiful Bria Jones if she had change for a twenty-dollar bill. She then gave Norris and Quentin their signal at the bar, which was to tip the bartender five dollars before she gave Tyrone change for a twenty. She left the club shortly afterward and walked toward the getaway car that was parked a few blocks down the street as opposed to the parking lot, and all of them entered the club separately just in case anyone was taking notice.

Max took another puff of his cigar and put it out in an empty glass on the table nearest to him. Illinois is a smoke-free state, so he made sure not to smoke too long, so one of the bouncers wouldn't approach him. He then looked at a guy's watch that read seven minutes after twelve and motioned toward the bathroom to claim the first stall.

"Showtime," he whispered to himself.

18

A tall, broad-shouldered man answered the door and searched Tommy Glenn before allowing him to enter the mansion. He first looked up at the twelve-foot high ceiling, and then he marveled at the HD television hanging from the wall, the leather sofa set and reclining chair that was right in front of him. The entire living room area had hardwood flooring that led to a bathroom to the immediate right, a fully-stocked bar farther back, a kitchen, dining room, and three bedrooms on the main level. Cedric was sitting on the sofa watching the Cubs play the Mets at Wrigley Field.

"Have a seat," Cedric said. "The Cubs better get it together because the Brewers are for real this year."

"I haven't had a chance to check them out yet this year," Tommy G said.

"Let's get right to it then. What the hell happened out there, Tommy?"

"Tyrone set us up. Tyrone and his crew killed everybody and took the money and dope."

"If they killed everybody, you wouldn't be sitting here telling me the story. Tell me this. How did your whole crew get wasted in your crib, and you're still breathing?"

"I, uh...I was in the bathroom when I heard gunshots, so I jumped out the window..."

"You're kidding me, right? That was a coward's way out."

"I'm sorry, Uncle Ced. I didn't mean for anything to happen."

"Don't even sweat that, nephew," Cedric said, placing his hand on Tommy G's shoulder. "You've made me a ton of money over the years, and you're my sister's son, God rest her soul. I promised her I'd look after you before she died, and that's why I'm not gonna kill you. I brought you here because I wanna help you get outta town before the police find you. I know you wouldn't snitch on the family, but I can't risk this coming back to me in any way."

"You don't have to worry about a thing, Uncle Ced," Tommy G said, breathing a sigh of relief. "I wouldn't tell the cops nothing."

"I want you to go to Baton Rouge and lay low for a while. My wife's brother owns an apartment complex down there—I'mma need you to give him a hand with whatever he needs for a few months, and then you're on your own."

"Sure, no problem. Anything you need, I'm there for you, Unc."

"You're leaving tonight, and Stevens is gonna take you there. You're out the drug game for good. And one more thing..."

"What's that, Unc?"

"Mark my words, Tyrone will be dealt with."

The car was waiting for Tommy G in front of the house. He gave Cedric a hug and hopped in the back seat of the Lincoln town car. There was a full moon in the partly cloudy night sky as they drove off toward Interstate Fifty-Seven. It was the last time he would see Country Club Hills or Chicago for that matter. He had the next fifteen hours to reflect on that fact.

He grabbed a beer out of the mini fridge in the back of the car and took a big gulp. He was grateful to be getting a fresh start in a new town, and he couldn't wait to put Chicago in his rearview mirror.

It finally sunk in that he'd be dead if his boss wasn't his uncle, and the fact that the police wanted to question him about the murders at his house would only be a formality if they ever found him. He could easily say that he had no idea what happened—there was no solid evidence to suggest that he was even there that night, since his whole crew was dead, or he could say he loaned out his house to friends while he was out of town. If the police ever caught up with Tyrone, it would be his word against Tyrone's word—a battle he'd probably win because of his uncle. He luckily didn't have a criminal record because of his uncle's connections, and his only brush with the law was spending a night in jail for a DUI. He got probation and community service for it.

He took another gulp and finished his beer before looking out the tinted window to his right and saw nothing but cornfield and darkness. He was fast asleep once his fear of being in jail or dead was gone.

19

Max removed the Glock from under the toilet and waited. The restroom was somewhat crowded with no other available stalls at the moment. Quentin, Tyrone, and Norris had come inside shortly after Max did, and they both stood by idly until the next stall became available. There was a steady influx of people in and out of the restroom, and the club was filled to capacity. Stall three opened up, and Quentin went inside. That left stall two and four occupied by guys who weren't part of the crew.

The fourth stall opened up a few seconds later, and Tyrone went in. Norris continued to wait patiently until stall two finally opened up. Norris then went in and promptly shut the door. He tried not to let the smell overpower him as he grimaced as if in excruciating pain. He then reached under the toilet and removed the last Glock before sitting down. Several seconds later, he reached in his pocket and pulled out his black mask to put on. He then gave the final signal of their elaborate scheme, which was the distinct sound of three taps on the stall door with the barrel of his gun.

Max was the first to storm out with his gun in the air, and Quentin, Tyrone, and Norris followed suit. They all heard screams, and everyone in their path literally parted the Red Sea for them, while others scurried toward the front cntrance.

"Blaka, blaka, blaka!" Max had shot one of the bouncers by the door of the office in the chest twice.

The other bouncer lunged at Max, and Quentin tried to empty his clip in bouncer number two's body after Max hit the floor, "Blaka, blaka, blaka, blaka, blaka, blaka, blaka, blaka, blaka!"

The remaining four bouncers zoomed in on the crew, and Tyrone and Norris shot all four of them and a couple of patrons in the process as pandemonium permeated the club. Max jumped to his feet and kicked open the office door with Tyrone right behind him. Norris and Quentin brought up the rear and guarded the area with his back to the door—aiming his gun at anyone who so much as blinked at them once they reached the top of the stairs.

"Get the outta the way!" Max shouted, hitting Wesley in the head with the barrel of his gun.

"Aw, damn," Wesley howled, hitting the floor and holding the side of his head where Max bludgeoned him.

"Let's load up!" Tyrone exclaimed, flapping the garbage bag that he pulled out of his pocket in the air.

Max and Tyrone hastened to empty the bundles of hundreds, fifties, and twenties in their respective bags, while Wesley tried to get up off the floor but fell back down. He tried to focus once the blurriness began to subside and recognized Max's tattoo of a dragon on his right forearm in addition to remembering his voice.

"Fifteen seconds!" Norris shouted, looking at his watch. "Come on, fellas, we gotta bail!"

"Give me your garbage bag, Norris!" Max shouted. "My bag is full."

"Here!" Norris exclaimed as he handed Max the empty bag with his free hand while still wielding his gun at the crowd.

"I know who the hell you are," Wesley said.

"What you say?" Max asked tersely.

"You're Mitch's boy, Gary," Wesley answered. "Don't you know that this is his club you're robbing?"

"Come on, man. We gotta bounce," Quentin urged.

Max raised his mask above his eyebrows and said, "See you in hell, Wes."

Max let off three more shots—two shots to Wesley's chest and one to his head. Max lowered his mask and grabbed one bag full of money, Tyrone grabbed his stuffed bag, and Norris grabbed the last bag before they all fled out the back door. Bria was waiting for them by the back entrance, and they sped off, exiting the rear entrance of the parking lot.

"Woohoo!" Norris shouted. "We hit the motherlode of jackpots, dammit!"

"Great job, guys," Bria said.

"I couldn't have pulled this score off without y'all," Quentin added. "You did good, too, Bria."

"Thank you, baby," Bria said.

"Way to quarterback things, cuz," Tyrone said. "I'm gettin' the hell outta dodge."

"You kinda quiet over there, Max," Quentin said. "You all right?"

"Yeah, man, I'm cool," Max answered. "That was my man's cousin Wes—I wasn't expecting him to be there."

"Don't even worry about that, Max," Quentin said. "You did what you had to do."

"Don't get me wrong," Max added. "There wasn't any love lost between us. He must have recognized my voice or something."

"I heard him say something about you robbing his cousin's club, didn't he?" Norris asked.

"Yeah, that's what he said," Max answered. "I had no idea Mitch owned that club."

"That was Mitch's cousin?" Tyrone asked. "Damn man, what are the odds of that happening?"

"I know, right?" Max asked rhetorically. "And that's what threw me off."

"Anyway, head on over to the spot, so we can burn this piece of junk," Quentin instructed Bria.

"Alright, baby," Bria said.

Quentin lit a cigarette while riding shotgun, and Bria checked her speed to make sure she wasn't driving over the limit. Max, Tyrone, and Norris were scrunched up in the back seat and couldn't wait for the ride to end. Bridgeview and every other suburb in that area were notorious for stopping people, even if they were one mile over the speed limit. The plan was to find a remote spot outside city limits and burn the car—no fingerprints, no evidence, and no witnesses who could link them to the robbery.

The transition vehicle was parked a couple of miles from the club and was an SUV with plenty of room. Quentin and Bria got out and hopped inside the Ford Explorer, and Tyrone got behind the wheel and followed them to a darkened, wooded area off LaGrange Road. They burned the getaway car deep in the woods and headed back to Max's apartment on South Shore Drive. The tentative plan was to settle up at Quentin's store the following day in the late morning. However, it wasn't written in stone because Quentin had other pressing business to tend to that morning and didn't know how long it was going to take. Once they arrived at Max's apartment, Max wanted to talk to Quentin in private while the rest of them waited inside the truck.

"Lemme holla at you for a second," Max said.

"What's up?" Quentin asked.

"We got ten *birds* that we need to unload, and I don't know who I can sell them to. Mack says you only sling heroin, so I wondering if you knew of somebody who slings cocaine."

"Nah, I don't really mess with cocaine, but I know of a dude out south that might take 'um off your hands. His name is Flip, and I've done biz with him in the past. I'll give him a call if you want me to."

"Is this dude on the up-and-up, homeboy?" Max asked, raising an eyebrow.

"As far as I know, Flip is legit," Quentin answered, putting his arm around Max. "He's independent and gets his product from Tijuana, I heard. It's like nobody ever heard of this guy, and boom, he just came outta nowhere."

"He ain't the Feds, is he?"

"Nah, I don't think so, but check him out if you're not sure. I've done biz with him a few times, and I'm still standing, bro."

"Yeah, I hear you. I really don't like to mess with dudes out south because most of them buy wholesale from Cedric. That guy I just killed used to be one of the biggest dope dealers out south, and he had a truce with Cedric. They had the whole south side sewn up from Cermark to 130th Street."

"You said his name was Wes, right?"

"Yeah, he used to break his cousin Mitch off when we were at TSU back in the day. I was Mitch's teammate and roommate, and let's just say that we rotated chicks in and out of our crib every day of the week."

"What y'all play?"

"We were on the basketball team together."

"That's what's up. So, money wasn't a problem as long as Wes was bank rolling y'all, huh?"

"No doubt, and Wes couldn't stand me because he thought I was using Mitch."

"Were you?"

"Nah, man, it wasn't even like that at all. Selling weed was my hustle, and I would steal anything I could get my hands on. Mitch is my man, one hundred grand, fam."

"I feel you, bruh. So, whatcha want me to do about Flip?"

"Set it up for me."

"Alright, see you later."

"Peace, Q."

20

Mitch and Brea lay sound asleep wrapped in each other's arms. Mitch's phone suddenly rang, and her clock read almost one o'clock. Mitch then jumped up and said, "Brea, what time is it?"

"Huh, baby?" she groaned.

"Damn, I gotta go—it's one o'clock. Was that my phone ringing?"

"I don't know...I think so."

His phone rang again. He picked it up on the first ring.

"Hello," he said.

"Where the hell are you, Mitch?" Sam asked. "You have to get here now!"

"Calm down, Sam. What's wrong?"

"We got robbed, man!"

"What? Was anybody hurt?"

"I'll tell you when you get here—there are cops everywhere."

"Alright, I'm on my way."

Mitch disconnected the call and jumped out of bed. He ran to the living room area to retrieve the rest of his clothes.

"What happened?" Brea asked.

"The club got robbed, and that's all I know."

"I'm coming with you."

"Nah, baby, that's not a good idea. There are cops all over the place, and I'm sure they're gonna ask me a ton of questions."

"You're right. I'm sorry."

"You don't have to apologize. I'll call you the moment I know what's going on, okay?"

"Alright, baby."

He kissed her once he got dressed and ran out the door to his car. He was on the expressway in about a minute as all six traffic lights between Brea's place and the Dan Ryan Expressway were green. He was in Bridgeview in about thirty minutes and at the club five minutes after that. There were police cars everywhere, and there were two ambulances parked in front of the entrance. His heart dropped to the ground when he saw the paramedics wheel a body out with the white sheet over its head.

He jumped out of his car and ran over to the ambulance where the body was. He prayed that it wasn't anyone he knew.

"Excuse me," Mitch said. "I'm the owner of this club—can I see who the body is?"

"We really need to get to the hospital, sir," one of the paramedics said.

"Please, ma'am?" Mitch asked.

"It's okay," the other paramedic said.

The male paramedic pulled back the sheet, and Mitch saw that it was his bouncer Tiny. He put his hand over his mouth in complete shock and leaned on the gurney to keep from falling on the ground.

"Do you know the decreased, sir?" the male paramedic asked.

"Yes, sir, he was one of my bouncers," Mitch answered.

"I'm sorry for your loss, sir," the female paramedic said.

"Thank you," Mitch said.

Mitch walked briskly inside the club not knowing what to expect next. The inside was a complete disaster area—tables turned over, broken glasses and bottles everywhere, and he noticed yellow tape by the office door.

"Oh, no!" Mitch yelled hysterically, running up the stairs toward the office.

"You can't go in there, sir!" one of the police officers shouted.

"Where's Wesley!" Mitch screamed. "Where's my cousin!"

Sam heard Mitch from the VIP room and came out to calm him down. He had been answering one of the policeman's questions about the robbery and shootings. Sam grabbed Mitch and restrained him before the policeman who told him not to enter the office came upstairs.

I'm sorry, Mitch," Sam said. "He's gone—they took him away a few minutes before you got here. I didn't want to tell you over the phone."

"What?" Mitch asked. "He's dead?"

"Yeah, man, I'm sorry."

"Oh, God! No!"

Mitch fell to his knees and began wailing uncontrollably. Sam knelt down and put his hand on his back in an attempt to console him for a few minutes and helped him back up off the floor.

"It's gonna be all right, Mitch," Sam said. "I'm here if you need anything."

"Thanks, Sam," Mitch said, wiping the stream of tears from his face and trying to regain his composure. "So, how did this happen?"

"I don't really know—everything happened so fast. All I heard was gunshots, and the crowd went bananas. They literally destroyed the place, and a couple of patrons got shot."

"Did they die?"

"I don't know..."

"Great—that's just great. We're probably going to be sued in addition to being robbed. So, tell me this, how much did they get?"

"All of it—tonight's money plus the money in the safe."

"Damn, man, can the night get any worse? They hit us for over a million, Sam."

"What? We gotta find out who hit us tonight. We can't let them just get away with..."

"No, Sam, we're going to let the police handle this. I can't afford to lose you or anybody else. Once we clean this place up, we're getting metal detectors and cameras."

"My bad, you're absolutely right."

"Look, man, in spite of how messed up things are at this moment, I like the way you handled things tonight. I'm going to need you to step up now that Wes is gone. I'm also going to need some time off to bury him and Tiny."

"It wasn't just them—our entire security team was wiped out tonight, Mitch..."

"What?! Ugh! How did these guys get guns in here, anyway?!"

"I don't know that, either. The police found duct tape in the men's room, though. Whoever snuck the guns in here taped them under the toilets."

"This is so jacked up on so many levels, Sam. I'm about to lose my damn mind!"

"Calm down, Mitch. If you need some extra time to bury your cousin and clear your head, take all the time you need. I got things covered here, so you don't have to worry about anything."

A despondent Mitch then gathered his thoughts and said, "I know this isn't really the time to talk about this, but Wes wouldn't want us to wallow in self-pity. I need you to be my partner when all the smoke clears. You're the only person I can trust, Sam."

"I would be honored, but you're right. This isn't the time to discuss this. Just focus on getting yourself together—allow yourself some time to grieve."

The policeman came out of VIP and said, "I think we have everything we need for now, Mr. Waters. If we have any more questions, we'll call you."

"Okay," Sam said.

"Excuse me, officer," Mitch said. "I'm the owner of the club. Do you need me to answer any questions or fill out any paperwork?"

"Were you present when the shooting took place?" the officer asked.

"No, sir," Mitch answered.

"Give me your name and number," the officer said, "and we'll contact you if we have more questions. In the meantime, you can stop by the station at your earliest convenience and file a police report."

"Thank you, officer," Mitch said, shaking his hand.

Mitch gave the officer one of his cards, and Mitch and Sam went to the VIP room to continue their conversation. Mitch poured himself a drink and sat down on the sofa.

"I need to call my wife and let her know what happened tonight," Mitch said.

"Do you want me to call Marisol, too?" Sam asked.

"Nah, I'll take care of it. She should hear it from me that Wes was killed tonight—she's family. I'm just worried how little Wesley is going to take it."

"I understand."

"Can you close up everything when the cops are done? I need to get out of here."

"Yeah, I got you covered. Here, take my keys and go to my crib. You need to clean yourself up if you know what I mean."

"Huh? Oh yeah, thanks, man. Sandra would kill me if she knew where I really was tonight. I just can't deal with that right now."

"No problem, Mitch. You're a grown man, and you don't owe me any explanations."

21

Quentin was lounging around on Sunday afternoon when his doorbell rang. He wasn't expecting any company and had already settled up with the guys that morning. He was watching the White Sox pound on the Angels and sipping on a beer before getting up to answer the door. He saw Bria through the peephole and opened the door to let her in. She was smoking a cigarette and was half-naked with a white tube top, daisy dukes, and Chanel sandals. She loved to wear next to nothing or nothing at all—and she undoubtedly had the body for it. She had danced at *Club Ecstasy* for just two weeks before quitting—just long enough to pull off the job of sneaking the pistols inside the men's bathroom.

"I told you to call first before poppin' up on me," Quentin barked. "I'm not your damn man."

"I know you're not my man, Quentin," Bria retorted after blowing smoke out of her nostrils. "I'm here for my cut of the money. We were on the freakin' national news this morning."

"I got your damn money, girl. Just chill out, all right?"

"Alright then, that's better. How much did we manage to get our hands on last night, and why didn't you tell me y'all were gonna settle up this morning?"

"It was a slower night than we anticipated, and I don't owe you any explanations on how I conduct business, Bria. We only cleared a little over five hundred thousand, so your cut is fifty grand..."

"That's not what we agree upon—y'all only getting five hundred grand doesn't have anything to do with me, Quentin! My cut is still the same!"

"You're getting fifty grand—take it or leave it!"

"The hell I will! I took all the risk planting those guns in there, and I was the getaway driver. You said we were going to hit them for a least a million, so my cut is still two hundred grand. You can split the remaining three hundred grand with your crew."

"Bria, what the hell have you been smokin', huh? We already settled up this morning. You better take this fifty grand and bounce, woman."

"You think you're slick, don't you? Just give me my money so I can get the hell outta here."

Quentin got up and went to his bedroom to get her cut while she took the last puff of her cigarette before putting it out in an ashtray on the coffee table. He reemerged a few seconds later and handed her five bundles of one-hundred-dollar bills.

"Here, babe," he said. "Why don't you lemme get in them shorts?"

"Go to hell!" she shouted. "You will never hit this again."

"Get outta my house, trick."

She stormed out the door and slammed it shut. He laughed out loud to himself and sat back down on the couch. Afterwards, he grabbed the remote and started flicking channels.

"Stupid 'ho," he said to himself.

22

"Hold all my calls, Connie," Mitch said. "I've got a ton of work to do."

"Sure thing, Mr. Black," Connie said. "If I haven't told you before, I'm very sorry about your cousin. I wish I could've been there for his funeral. Let me know if you need anything, okay?"

"Thanks, I will. How was your vacation?"

"We had the time of our lives in Hawaii."

"That's great, Connie."

"Well, I'm going to get back to work."

Connie walked out of his office, and he soon busied himself in paperwork. He worked feverishly throughout the entire morning and well into the afternoon. He thought, if he kept himself totally occupied, his mind wouldn't constantly be on Wesley.

His guilt for not being there when Wesley got killed at the club was taking its toll on him. He also felt he should've died with him because his life was spared because he was cheating on his wife with Brea. His cell phone rang, and he thought about not answering it, but the area code was a 212 prefix. He knew it was Jada, so he took the call.

"Hi, Jada, how have you been?" Mitch asked.

"I'm fine, Mitch," Jada answered. "I'm just settling in. I heard about Wesley—I'm so sorry, baby."

"Thank you, sweetheart—thanks for checking up on me."

"Are you okay? Do you need me to do anything for you?"

"Nah, I'm all right. Just you calling me makes me feel a whole lot better."

"Once I get my place together, I'll send you a plane ticket to come see me. I'm in Manhattan, and the view here is crazy."

"I'd like that, Jada. Well, thanks for calling. I would like to talk longer, but I've got a mountain of paperwork to catch up on."

"Oh, okay, I won't keep you. Take care, baby, and call me if you need anything."

"I will. Bye."

"Bye."

He disconnected the call, and before he could get back to work, there was a knock at his office door. Sandra came in before he could say anything, and he got up to greet her with a hug and a kiss. He'd been very distant since the robbery, and she thought it would be best if she helped him out of his funk, rather than giving him his space. Truth be told, he was being comforted by Brea whenever he had free time over the past several weeks. Burying himself in work at the firm and at the club was just a cover to spend more time with her. He didn't realize he was neglecting one relationship while nurturing another one.

"I thought I could pull you away for a little while and grab some lunch," Sandra said. "Have you eaten yet?"

"No, baby, I haven't had time," Mitch answered. "I'll just get something out of the vending machine when I get a chance."

"That's not real food, Mitch. You need to eat something—come on, let's go to Ruth's Chris Steakhouse."

"I said I can't, Sandra. Why are you down here, anyway?"

"Well, excuse the hell outta me for caring, Mr. Black. And for your information, I'm down here to register for school, remember? Oh, wait, why would you remember—you never have time for me anymore."

"That's not fair, Sandra. You know I just lost my cousin, and all you can think about is yourself. I need some time, baby—I need time to sort things out, okay?"

"Take all the time you need, Mitch. I'm out."

"You're out? What does that mean?"

"It's means I'm going to get some business since you got so much business of your own going on."

Sandra walked out, and Mitch took off his reading glasses and sighed. He was relieved when she left the office because he really didn't have the patience to listen to her blab about her friends and family over lunch. When he wasn't thinking about Wesley, he was thinking about Brea. He was in way over his head and couldn't do anything to stop the snowball from rolling down the slope.

23

"Now that you got your money, what are you gonna do?" Tyrone asked.

"Me and Jill are gonna move down south," Max replied. "I got that deal set up with Quentin's man Flip tomorrow, too. He's gonna take them *birds* off our hands for 100K—that's an extra thirty-three grand in our pockets."

"Do you need me to watch your back tomorrow?"

"Yeah, and I'm gonna need another favor from you, too."

"No problem, what is it?"

"I checked out Flip's resume, and I'mma need an extra man for my plan. I'll fill you in later."

"Aiight, I got you, Max. Say, what part of the south are y'all moving to?"

"Jill got peoples in Louisiana, so I'mma set up shop down there—a barbershop near the Southern University campus—and I'm gonna open up a carwash eventually. You should come, too. We can be partners."

"I'm in, homeboy. Lemme get on that extra man for you. I'm out."

"Peace, my brother."

"Peace."

They gave each other a fist thump, and Tyrone left Max and Jill's apartment. Jill came in the living room with two beers and sat down on the sofa next to Max.

"You packed yet, babe?" Max asked.

"Yes, baby, we're set to go," Jill answered. "We're off to our new life. Thank you for keeping your promise to me. You know that I'm down for whatever, but we have to go legit for our son."

"I totally agree with you one hundred percent. I've done a hell of a lot of dirt in my life, but I feel it's never too late to change. Here's to our new life."

"To our new life. Cheers, baby."

"Cheers."

They tapped bottles and snuggled up to each other. She kissed him on the cheek and said, "I love you, Gary."

"I love you, too, babe. Once I unload these *birds*, we can leave town tomorrow."

"Be careful. What do you know about this guy?"

"I know everything I need to know about him. Don't worry about it, okay?"

"I know you can handle yourself out here, Gary. Just make sure you make it back here to us."

"I'm always extra cautious. Everything is gonna work out, I promise."

24

Mitch had made a pit stop at Brea's before heading to the club. It had been his routine every day since the robbery and Wesley's murder to stop by her place after work before putting in his hours at *Club Ecstasy*. He had only taken off a couple of days to make funeral arrangements and to bury his cousin. She would always prepare a home-cooked meal for him, followed by wild, passionate lovemaking, and she literally replaced Sandra in the number one spot in his life.

He stopped at the florist and bought her twelve long-stem, red roses, and he stopped at the liquor store and picked up a bottle of Hennessy. It was a little past six o'clock when he arrived at her place. She had given him his own key, so he parked his car and let himself in.

"Hey, baby," he said as he handed her the roses and placed the bottle of Hennessy on the kitchen counter and kissed her.

"Thank you, sweetie," she said. "I'll put these in water."

"Damn, I could smell the food a half-block away, and I'm starving."

"I have to make sure my king is well-fed. So, how was your day?"

"My wife stopped by to take me to lunch this afternoon."

"Really? Where did you all go?"

"We didn't go out anywhere—I told her I was busy, and we got into a fight."

"I see. You should've took her out, anyway—she's going to start to suspect something, Mitch."

"I know, but I really was too busy. Besides, as crazy as this sounds, I felt like I'd be cheating on you if I went out with her. Imagine that."

"Are you for real, baby?"

"I wouldn't lie to you—I couldn't lie to you if I tried. I never knew how real love felt until I met you, Brea. I'm crazy about you."

"I'm crazy about you, too, Mitch."

Brea put her spatula on the stove and wrapped her arms around Mitch's shoulders before passionately kissing him. She let go of her embrace and said, "Where do we go from here?"

"I want us to be like this every day," he answered. "The problem is I'm still married. One thing is for certain; we can't go on like this."

"What are you saying? Are you going to tell her the truth?"

"Yes, but I don't know how I'm going to break the news to her."

"I don't want to pressure you, but I'm not going to lie either. You're about to go through hell for a minute because no woman ever wants to hear that her husband is leaving her for another woman."

"I don't feel any pressure when I'm with you—you've been a godsend to me ever since Wes was murdered. I don't know where I'd be without you."

"I'm just glad I can be here for you, and I'm going to take good care of you from now on."

She finished preparing their dinner, they ate, they laughed, and they cuddled on the sofa after finishing their meal. One thing led to another, and thirty minutes into watching television, the television was watching them. Nothing else mattered whenever they hooked up from Monday through Sunday. Their evening escapades continued in the bedroom, and it was time for him to go to the club before they knew it.

"I hate that I have to go," he said.

"Why don't you stay then?" she asked.

"You know I can't do that. I can't afford to be an absentee boss anymore now that Wes is gone."

"I know, but you can't blame a girl for trying."

"Don't worry. We'll be spending every night together very soon."

"I'll wait for you—no matter how long it takes."

"I promise I won't make you wait too long."

"Will I see you tomorrow?"

"Of course you will."

"I'll cook you something very special."

"Damn, girl, you're gonna make me fat as hell..."

"Don't worry, I'll make sure you work it off."

He got out of bed and headed to the bathroom to take a shower. She ironed his clothes that were on the bedroom floor and packed him some food just in case he got hungry later. It was almost ten o'clock when he came out the bedroom to leave.

"I'll call you on my way home from the club," he said, kissing her on the cheek.

"You're the hardest working man I've ever met," she said. "When are you going to slow down?"

"I'll slow down when I'm old. As long as there's money to be made, I'm gonna make it. How's your record deal coming?"

"It's at a standstill right now—that jerk Calvin had my hopes up pretty high. All he wanted was some sex—he had no intention on helping me out. Maybe I'll go back to New York to make it happen."

"You're thinking about leaving me? Damn, I don't know how I'm going to deal with that, baby."

"Relax, I'm was just thinking out loud; that's all. I will never leave you, Mitch—I still have my paintings to consider. I'm entering an art show next month."

"That's wonderful, Brea. I'll make sure all your paintings get sold. I can have everybody at the firm buy a piece."

"You'd do that for me? Wow, you-are-so-incredible."

"I'll do anything for you. Don't you know that by now?"

"Yes, baby, I do."

25

Bria was waiting to meet Cedric at a soul food restaurant on Seventy-Fifth Street near the Dan Ryan Expressway. She had ordered a cup of coffee and a slice of pie before he arrived. She desperately wanted to smoke a cigarette but chose something sweet to eat and caffeine as way to deal with her impatience.

Bria Jones was a sociopath, who could kill someone at a moment's notice and not give it a second thought. The death of her parents traumatized her to the point of displaying degenerate behavior as a way to cope with her pain. Like Brea, she used her sexuality as a weapon to get what she wanted from men, but she also partook in criminal activities as a subconscious way of dealing with her issues.

Cedric entered the restaurant and searched for Bria. Not small in stature at six-foot-three, he had a presence about him that signified someone of extreme importance and someone not to be disrespected in any way. Bria then stood up and greeted Cedric with a hug once he spotted her seated in the corner of the restaurant.

"Long time no see, Bria," Cedric said.

"Yes, it has been a long time," Bria said.

"So, what's up?"

"I need you to take care of somebody for me. This guy thinks he's gonna short me on my money, but he's got another thing coming."

"I can do that for you. Where does he stay?"

"Out west—he owns a corner store in K-Town. I gave him the inside track on robbing this club in Bridgeview several weeks ago. I also helped him get the guns in there, and now he's trying to play me."

"That was y'all? Damn, that heist was off the hook, girl. I used to sling for the dude's uncle who got killed. Yeah—Wes and I go way back. We came up in the game together, and we took over the south side after his uncle got life in prison for murder and racketeering. He got out the game last year and opened up that club."

"Hey, I didn't know—I didn't know you knew Wes. They were only supposed to rob the club, not kill anybody."

"I don't blame you, and we weren't on good terms, anyway. Karma was bound to catch up to him one day."

"Oh, okay. So, how much do you want?"

"Even though me and Wes had our differences, he was still like family to me. Because of that, I'll do this dude for free. What's his name?"

"His name is Quentin Adams, and he got a cousin named Tyrone. Everybody calls him Mack, though."

"You say his name is Tyrone Mack?"

"Yeah, you know him?"

"Yeah, I know him."

"Well, do me a favor and let Quentin know that I sent you before you put his lights out."

"No doubt, girl. How's Brea doing?"

"She's good. I'll tell her you asked about her."

"Is she still trying to sing? That girl knows she can blow."

"Yeah, as far as I know she is. She got a new man, too, and he owned that club with Wes. I think his name is Mick—nah—his name is Mitch."

"Damn, it's a small world. I've known Mitch just as long as I've known Wes. Does he know that he's got his hands full with your sister?"

"Huh? No, Brea didn't have anything to do with this, Cedric."

"Yeah, I bet. Look, I'll take care of that business for you; give Brea my best."

"Thanks, Cedric, I owe you."

"Nah, you don't owe me anything, Bria. Just watch your back out here."

"I will. Take care."

Cedric left, and Bria pulled her cell phone from her purse. She dialed Brea's number, and she answered on the first ring.

"Baby, is that you?" Brea asked, waking up from her deep sleep.

"No, silly, it's me," Bria answered. "Mitch's got your nose wide open."

"What do you want, Bria?"

"I just talked to your ex—he's gonna take care of Quentin for shorting me on my money."

"I don't want to know anything about it, girl. Just promise me that you will be careful, okay?"

"You know me—I know what time it is out here, Brea. I think Cedric still has a thing for you, though."

"I could really care less about him—he had his chance, but he couldn't stop cheating on me with all of his other side chicks."

"You were his mistress, Brea. I still don't understand why you still trippin' about that. You could've kept taking Cedric's money, but you fell in love. You shouldn't have cared about who else he was sleeping with."

"You just don't get it—I'm not playing the third or fourth fiddle to anybody. I have too much respect for myself."

"Whatever, sis. All they ever want is sex anyway, so you might as well get paid for it. If you weren't my sister, I'd slap some sense into you."

"I'm about to hang this phone up on you, Bria..."

"Girl, you are too funny. I'll see you tomorrow."

"Okay, see you tomorrow. Bye."

Bria ended the call and got up to pay her bill. Guys seated throughout the diner stared in lust as she strutted toward the door in her six-inch, leopard-print stilettos and black miniskirt with leopard print around the shoulder area that showed off her sexy body. She favored Brea a great deal, but she was slightly shorter and a shade lighter.

"Why don't you lemme holla at you for a minute, gorgeous," a guy said, standing on the curb next to her car.

"I would, but you can't afford me, sweetheart," she answered.

"Stuck up trick," he retorted.

"Whatever," she barked. "Move away from my car."

"What?" he asked, inching his way toward her.

"Back-the-hell-up, I said!" she shouted, pulling her two-shot Derringer from her purse and aiming it at his head.

“My bad, ma,” he said remorsefully, raising his hands in the air. “You got it.”

“I thought so,” she said, unlocking the doors of her black Corvette with her remote and driving off.

26

Mitch felt it was a good idea to stop by Marisol's to check up on her and his little cousin, Wesley Jr. He hadn't spoken to her since the funeral, and he wanted to give her the paperwork on all of Wesley's business dealings as promised. She had unanswered questions that he needed to clarify, and he had decided to come clean about everything. He owed her that much, he thought.

He parked in front of their house and rang the doorbell. She greeted him with a firm hug that lasted several moments before she released her embrace.

"How have you been, Marisol?" Mitch asked.

"It's getting a little better each day," Marisol answered, "but I'm still in a lot of pain. I don't know how I'm going to go on without him."

"I feel the same way—a day doesn't go by without me wondering how I could've done things differently."

"That's just it, Mitch. What the hell happened out there? You should've been watching his back."

"I know, and I feel guilty enough about it. I had gotten a call from a friend that night because she caught a flat tire on Lake Shore Drive. My plans were to fix her flat and get back to the club to help Wes count the money."

He paused, wiped his forehead, and said, "Once I fixed the flat, I told her I had to get back to the club, but she insisted on showing her gratitude by cooking me dinner. I didn't see the harm because I still had time, but one thing led to another, and we wound up in bed."

"Dammit, Mitch, why can't you keep it in your pants for once? I would've busted you out a long time ago if Sandra and I didn't dislike each other so much..."

"I know, Marisol—I'm sorry. He had always been there for me, and I didn't mean for any of this to happen."

She walked over to him and hugged him again, and she said, "You couldn't have known what was going to happen, and I don't blame you. Both of you would be dead if you had been at the club that night."

"Thank you, sis—it means a lot to hear you say that."

He let go of his embrace and said, "Wes set up a life annuity for you and a trust fund for little Wesley. I have all of the paperwork right here."

"Thank you, Mitch. You've been so good to us. Thank you for stepping up and handling all of the funeral arrangements."

"No problem, you're family. He also had some properties, a stock portfolio, and offshore accounts that he set up in both of your names. Here are the account numbers right here—he wanted you all to be set just in case something happened to him. And there's one more thing."

"What's this, Mitch?" she asked as Mitch handed her the small box.

"Wes had planned on marrying you on your birthday in a couple of months, and he would've wanted you to have this," he answered.

"Wow, I don't know what to say," she said, wiping tears from her eyes. "He was really going to marry me."

"You two were his world—you and little Wesley. He wanted to make it official. Well, I've got to head on over to the club."

"I appreciate you stopping by and thank you for telling me what really happened that night. You could've lied about it, but you didn't."

"I would never lie to you about something like that. Wes was more than just my cousin—he was my brother in every sense of the word. I'll see you soon, okay?"

"Okay. Take care."

"Goodbye, Marisol."

He kissed her on the cheek and walked out. He arrived at the club a little while later and greeted everyone at the front entrance near the bar before heading to the office upstairs. Sam had gotten metal detectors and cameras installed the week after the robbery, and business had begun to pick up again once patrons felt safe. He also hired an off-duty policeman to head security at the front entrance.

Mitch needed a moment to pull himself together before managing the floor the way Wesley used to do. He was a lot better at dealing with the public, while Wesley was better at managing the staff, but Wesley was only better at it because he had more experience. Mitch was a natural at running things, and it wasn't long before he felt completely comfortable doing it.

He spotted Sam by the bar and walked up to him. He was filling in nicely for Wesley, but Mitch still wanted to be more hands-on than he had been in the past.

"How's everything going?" Mitch asked.

"Things are starting to get back to normal," Sam answered, "and this is the busiest Monday we've had in a month. How are you feeling?"

"I'm starting to feel a little better each day—you know—one day at a time."

"I'm glad to hear that."

"I just want to tell that you're doing a great job, Sam. I can't run this place without you."

"Thanks for having confidence in me, Mitch."

"No problem, you earned it."

Mitch walked back to the VIP room to pour himself a drink and relax for a moment. He hadn't been able to book any celebrities for VIP since the robbery until he nabbed someone for Friday night. A local actor named Bobby Tran, who studied at Juilliard and starred in his first box office film, was slated to grace the club with his presence. His film was in the top ten for five weeks straight. Celebrities and their entourages were great moneymakers for the club, and their tabs ran into thousands of dollars for one night. Cedric stepped inside the club a few minutes later and was searched by security. Mitch came out of the room to greet Cedric once he spotted him.

"What brings you here, Ced?" Mitch asked.

"I came by to give my condolences for Wes," Cedric answered. "Even though we had our differences, I still consider both of you family."

"Thank you, Ced. It means a lot that you came by. So, what's the word on the streets?"

"I've got nothing, Mitch," he lied. "Some guys hit my best money-making crack house several weeks ago, but I don't know if it's all connected or not. They killed five of my men."

"All connected to what?" Mitch asked with a perplexed look.

"My crack house getting hit and your club."

"Come on man, Chicago is a big place. I doubt if one has anything to do with the other."

"You're right, Chicago is a big place, but it's not that big. Stuff like this just doesn't happen—I've been in this game far too long to know that."

"So, what are you saying is, the same guys who hit you hit me?"

"I don't know, maybe. Just be careful, man."

"I hear you, Ced. I heard about what happened over there on the news."

"Same here, I heard about your situation on the news, too."

"How's Tommy? Is he okay?"

"My nephew is safe, and that's all you need to know."

Mitch nodded, and they stood in silence for a moment before Mitch said, "Yo, Ced, thanks for coming by, man. If you want something to drink, tell my bartender I said your drinks are on the house tonight."

"Thanks, Mitch, I appreciate that, but there's one more thing I want to talk to you about."

"Yeah, what's that?"

"Word around town is you've been seeing a girl named Brea Jones. Is that true?"

"Oh yeah, who told you that?"

"A little bird."

"What's your point, Ced?"

"Stay away from her. She's bad news."

"I'm a big boy, man. I can take care of myself."

"I know you can take care of yourself, Mitch. You did good by staying in school and not in the streets. I'm just saying that I like the way you handle business, and messing with Brea can be hazardous to your health."

"How do you know so much about Brea?"

"Let's just say we used to be an item a while ago, but I realized she's poison."

"You really need to watch yourself, bruh. Remember, you're still a guest here."

"No disrespect, homeboy. She took me for a hell of a ride, but when the smoke cleared, I saw her for exactly who she was. When your blinders come off, you'll see what I mean."

"Why do you even care? You never struck me as the jealous type."

"I'm not," he lied again. "I found out you were seeing her right after your club got hit. Mighty big coincidence, don't you think?"

"I know you're not trying to blame the robbery on her, are you?"

"Do you have a wife?"

"Huh? What does that have to do with anything?"

"I said, do you have a wife?"

"Yeah, man, so what?"

"Let's just say that you better check under your car seats or bed for earrings or panties after hooking up with her. She has a way of making her presence known in the subtlest of ways, my friend."

"I'll make note of that," Mitch said sarcastically. "Go have that drink before I change my mind."

"Thanks, man, I will," Cedric laughed. "Take care."

"Um hum."

Cedric walked back toward the bar, and Mitch went back upstairs to VIP to pour himself another drink and think. He tried his best not to let Cedric get in his head by focusing on how he was going to tell Sandra about his relationship with Brea.

"No more lies and no more secrets from now on," he said to himself.

27

Max and Tyrone were on their way to Flip's warehouse in the south suburbs to make the deal. Flip owned a trucking company, and he hauled everything from canned goods to electronics from every part of the country. He would stash the marijuana and cocaine with each shipment that he brought to Chicago.

They all agreed to meet at six because business hours concluded at five thirty. Tyrone had been calling Quentin all day to inform him that the drug deal was going down in the evening at Flip's warehouse, but Quentin never answered.

"Damn, I've been trying to call Quentin all day, but he ain't answering," Tyrone said.

"Don't worry, Mack, I got everything covered," Max said reassuringly. "Quentin is probably tied up doing some business or something. Norris and your man are already on standby waiting for our signal."

"My gut is telling me that something ain't right, Max. He always answers my calls or texts."

"Aiight, we'll check on him after we meet up with Flip."

"Okay."

They arrived in Harvey at about ten minutes to six and parked in front of the warehouse moments later. Tyrone popped the trunk and grabbed the bag full of coke.

"You ready to do this?" Tyrone asked.

"Yeah, let's go inside," Max answered.

They walked toward the entrance, and Flip was waiting for them at the opening of the garage. He motioned for them to come inside and walked to the back of the warehouse.

"What's up, fellas," Flip said. "My name is Flip."

"I'm Max," he said, extending his hand to Flip, "and this is Mack."

"Nice to meet you both," Flip said. "Let's get down to business. You got ten keys for me, right?"

"Yep, got them right here," Tyrone answered. "Show us the money."

"I got the money here, but slow down a minute," Flip urged. "Quentin says you're cool, but I like to know who I'm dealing with."

"That's fair," Max said. "What do you wanna know, homeboy?"

"Where did y'all get that stash, and why are trying to unload it so fast, Max?" Flip asked. "I wanna make sure I'm not steppin' on somebody's toes. I can't afford no heat coming back to me."

"Everything is legit, Flip," Max answered. "We used to be into drugs, but we're out now. I'm moving out of Chicago for good, and I don't want no more ties to the game, you feel me?"

"Yeah, I feel you," Flip answered. "Wait here."

Flip went to his office and came out with a briefcase. One of his men standing a few yards away looked on while Flip opened the briefcase full of hundred-dollar bills.

"Wanna count it?" Flip asked.

"Nah, we trust you," Max said.

"Good," Flip said. "Nice doing business with you."

The men shook hands, and Max and Tyrone proceeded to walk out before being stopped in their tracks by Cedric and his men. The four of them had their guns drawn and aimed at Tyrone and Max. Max, Tyrone, Flip, and Flip's bodyguard subsequently drew their weapons on Cedric and his men.

"What the hell are you doing, Ced?" Flip asked angrily. "You are way out of bounds, my man."

"Chill out, Flip," Cedric said. "I'm here for these two murdering con artists."

"Get the hell outta here before I blast y'all!" Tyrone shouted.

"Everybody just relax," Max said calmly. "I don't wanna kill nobody, so let's put our guns down."

"As you can see, Ced, it looks like a stalemate," Flip said. "Nobody wants to die here—what is this about, anyway?"

"Put your guns down," Cedric said to his men. "I'm sorry for causing a ruckus, Flip, but these clowns robbed me and killed my men. I'm here to settle the score."

"Yeah?" Flip asked. "What the hell is going on, Max? A man ain't got a damn thing but his word when it all comes down to it."

"Forget him, Flip," Tyrone interjected. "He don't know what he's talking about."

"I should shoot you in the face right now, Big Ty," Cedric said. "Your cousin gave you up right before he begged for his life."

"What you say?" Tyrone asked, drawing his gun and aiming it at Cedric.

"You heard me," Cedric answered, drawing his gun and aiming at Tyrone.

Max and Flip's bodyguard drew their guns again and aimed them in Cedric's direction, and Cedric's men redrew their guns. However, Flip stood still.

"Put your gun down, Jerry," Flip urged his bodyguard. "This ain't got nothing to do with us."

"I'll let you in on another secret, Flip," Cedric said. "These two guys killed your man at that club a few weeks back. They robbed the club and shot him to death."

"What?" Flip asked, looking confused. "They were the ones who killed Wes?"

"Yeah, I killed Wes," Max said coldly. "He was an obstacle that had to be removed from the equation. It was business, nothing personal."

Flip then aimed his gun at Max and said, "Give me one good reason why I shouldn't kill you right now."

Max smiled and said, "You and your wife Tasha live at 801 East 162nd Street in South Holland, and Cedric's ex-wife Tracy and two sons, Justin and Douglas, live at 16501 South Kedzie Street in Markham. I have men at each one of your houses ready to blow their brains out if they don't get my signal in the next few minutes."

"Checkmate," Tyrone said.

Max continued, "We are going to walk outta here with this money, and y'all will never see us again. I suggest that you put your guns down now."

"Let's get the hell outta here," Cedric growled. "I'll see you soon, Tyrone—well done, Max."

Max nodded, and Cedric and his men left. Max turned to Flip and asked, "Are we cool, man?"

"Yeah, we're cool," Flip answered. "Jerry, show these gentlemen to the door."

Flip's bodyguard walked them to the entrance and stared at them while they hastened to their car. They slowly drove off, and Max never took his eyes off his rearview mirror until they were a safe distance away from the warehouse.

"You are always two steps ahead, Max," Tyrone said. "How the hell did you know this was gonna play out like that?"

"I didn't know," Max answered, "but I always play the percentages. I knew it was a good chance that Quentin's girl was gonna talk because he shorted her on her cut. And I did my homework too—I found out that all of them used to run in the same circle—Cedric, Flip, Wes, and that broad Bria."

"Damn, you're right. I should've known he cheated her when he said he was gonna pay her outta his cut."

Max paused and said, "I'm sorry about your cousin, though. I didn't anticipate him getting killed, man."

"Thanks, Max. It hurts, but I gotta charge it to the game. I don't know how Norris is gonna take it, though."

"We'll be there for him, but we'll have to convince him that going to war with Cedric isn't an option."

"He's gonna want to murder everyone responsible, Max. He's a loose cannon when backed into a corner."

"He'll listen to reason once he calms down. He knows he can't go up against Cedric by himself."

"Maybe you're right, and there nothing really keeping us all here, anyway."

"You're absolutely right. Let's just get the hell outta dodge, homeboy."

"When are we leaving?"

"As soon as Norris gets to my crib, we can all leave out together. Jill's peoples got a six-room house they built from the ground up in Baton Rouge. We can stay there for a few weeks until we find our own spots."

"Cool. I'mma get me a one or two-bedroom apartment for starters. I need to lay low for a while and not draw any attention to myself."

"That's the lick—lay low and stack this money, man."

28

Mitch and Brea had agreed earlier in the day that it was time to tell Sandra the truth about their relationship. He headed straight home from work and planned on going to the club after breaking the news to his wife. He parked in the driveway next to Sandra's car. She ordinarily parked her car inside the garage, but she left it outside that particular evening.

He reached to put his key in the lock, but the door was already ajar. He saw suitcases on the floor when he stepped inside, and Sandra was talking on the phone in the living room.

"What is this?" Mitch asked. "You booked the trip already?"

Sandra hung up the phone and said, "No, Mitch, I'm leaving."

"Leaving? Where the hell are you going?"

"Home—I'm going back to Houston."

"Why?"

"You tell me," she said, tossing a Manila envelope on the floor in his direction.

He knelt down to pick it up and pulled out the pictures that were inside the envelope. He studied each one of the pictures of Brea and him holding hands at the mall, kissing in front of Navy Pier, and eating dinner at a nearby restaurant for starters. An astonished Mitch looked up at an irate Sandra with her arms folded.

"You hired a private investigator to spy on me?" he asked.

"No, I didn't," she answered.

"So, you didn't have anything to do with these pictures?"

"No, Mitch, maybe one of your tramps took them."

"I'm sorry, Sandra. I really am. Look, I'm not going to deny what I did or who I am anymore. As a matter of fact, that's why I'm home so early."

"Lucky me, I was hoping to be gone by the time you got here."

"Look, I know I dogged you, and I truly regret that. Wesley's death made me realize that I can't live this lie any longer. I'm not going to pretend like everything is peaches and cream..."

"You're not going to pretend? All I ever did was love you, Mitch. I left my family behind in Houston and followed you here to Chicago. I've shown you over and over how I feel about you."

"You're absolutely right. I can't deny that. But you have to admit that there's something missing. I want children, and you don't—you weren't honest about it. And you still don't know what you want to do with your life. I would've been happy with you staying home and raising our kids, but that's not the life you want."

"Don't try to turn this around on me—you just want me out here in no man's land, so you can trick on all the women you want. Was she worth it?"

"It's not like that, baby."

"Then what is it like, huh? Do you love her?"

"Yes, I have deep feelings for her."

"Wow, I guess what we've been doing for the last nine years has been a waste of time."

"That's not fair..."

"Not fair?! I'll tell you what's not fair! You cheated on me this entire relationship! I just looked the other way because I didn't want to admit the truth to myself. I knew about the other women in college, but I never said anything because you never brought your dirt home until now. I was cool as long as I didn't see it—as long as some woman never tried to front me off about you, it didn't matter. I realize now that I created this monster, but I also realize I don't have to deal with this madness anymore."

"I'm not asking you to, Sandra. If you want me to leave, I'll pack my stuff tonight."

"No, you stay. I'll leave. I'm going home for good, so you can have this house. I don't want anything to do with you right now, and my lawyer will be in touch."

She grabbed her suitcases and left. He sat on the couch still in a state of shock. He racked his brain trying to figure out which one of the dozens of women he encountered over the last year sent Sandra the pictures, but he came up with nothing.

29

Brea was sitting on her living room sofa sipping on a glass of Hennessy and watching music videos on BETJ when she heard a knock at the door. She jumped off the sofa to answer it like a giddy schoolgirl.

"Baby, is that you?" Brea asked.

"No, dammit, it's me," Bria answered.

"What the hell are you doing here, sis? You sure know how to rain on somebody's parade."

"Damn, you knew I was coming—you really know how to make a person feel welcome."

"I didn't mean it like that. I thought you were Mitch—he's breaking up with his wife tonight."

"Good for you, Brea. Pour me a glass of *Henny*, too."

Brea went to the kitchen to pour Bria her glass, and Bria made herself at home by kicking off her shoes and lying on the sofa.

"Move those feet of yours out the way," Brea said.

"Oh, my bad," Bria said.

"When did you get braids?"

"I got them done today."

"I like them—I might get some."

"Thanks, I can have my girl hook you up."

Brea paused and said, "So what scheme are you on now?"

"I ain't on nothing, girl—just stopping by to check up on you. I miss us hanging out and everything."

"I don't hang no more because you're always wildlin' out. We're getting older, and I don't have time for your shenanigans anymore."

"Don't give me that—you have time when you want me to do something for you."

"And I'm there for you, too, Bria—like the club—had I known you all were going to rob the place, I never would have agreed to do it."

"Yeah, and when I sent you to the club to check things out, you were supposed to find out who owned it, not sleep with one of them."

"Hell, Mitch is fine, and I knew he would be mine the first time I saw him. Thank God you gave me the heads-up when it all went down, or else Mitch would be dead, too."

"Um hum, and I wonder how Mitch would feel if he knew the truth, Brea?"

"He would probably feel like I was responsible for his cousin death, and that's why he can never know about any of this—do-you-feel-me, Bria?"

"You ain't gotta worry, sis—I'm not trying to incriminate myself. I gotta admit, though, flattening your own tire so that you could get him outta there was brilliant."

"I had to do something. My back was against the wall."

"And getting me to hire a private investigator to take pictures of y'all was brilliant, too. I bet his wife never saw *that* coming, and I never would have come up with something like that in a million years."

"Mitch needed a little extra push in the right direction, so I gave him one."

"Ooh, still the same old Brea, but I like it."

"I did it for love. How far would you go for the man you love?"

"I don't know, Brea. I guess I never really been in love."

"Well, I'll do anything for Mitch, and I'll take out anybody who gets in my way."

"On that note, I'mma pour myself another glass of Hennessy."

"Here, pour me one, too."

Bria held up her glass and said, "Here's to keeping secrets and protecting what's ours."

"Bottoms up," Brea added.

30

Six months later...

Mitch's life had been on a downward spiral since he split up with his wife Sandra, and things seemed to be getting worse with each passing day. His divorce had just been finalized, and the court ordered him to pay over five thousand dollars per month in alimony. This wouldn't have been a problem before getting fired from his day job and being audited by the IRS, but since most of his assets were presently frozen, making timely payments was going to be next to impossible. The only thing that saved him from paying more was the fact that he buried a good portion of his earnings in stocks, bonds, and mutual funds in his mother's name.

He was able to shake the Feds with his money laundering schemes that hid his dead cousin Wesley's drug money in real estate and stock, but he couldn't fool the IRS by trying to evade paying taxes on the millions of dollars in income the club earned the previous year. He was facing possible prison time, and the best-case scenario would be paying a hefty fine to the IRS.

He had just downed six shots of Jim Bean and was working on a beer to intensify his intoxication at a bar in the West Pullman area of town. He had hoped to get drunk enough to forget all his present problems, like the seizing of his half million-dollar home, his nightclub, and his ninety-thousand-dollar Mercedes Benz, but history always repeated itself when he would awaken with a hangover and nausea worse than a pregnant woman.

In addition to his financial woes, his relationship with Brea was on the rocks. They weren't constantly at each other's throats, but she had begun to spend less and less time with him. She was either at the studio recording tracks for her demo—or she was running the streets with her twin sister, Bria. Nevertheless, the option of spending time with Mitch wasn't very appealing to her anymore. He had, in fact, suspected her of cheating on him but couldn't actually prove it. She would vehemently deny any wrongdoing—one day, he tried to greet her with a kiss after she returned from partying, but she pulled away from him because she smelled like sex. He wanted to confront her about it, but he chose the option of letting it go because he knew he couldn't handle the truth yet. It was easier just to stick his head in the sand.

Mitch's mind was telling him to cut his losses and let Brea go, but his heart said otherwise. The thought of losing her made him even more depressed than he already was because he had given up everything to be with her—giving his heart completely to her, thinking it was completely safe in her possession—but he would quickly learn that she was a narcissist, who could turn her feelings on and off like a light switch.

He even contemplated suicide, but divine intervention saved him from eternal damnation. An 80-pack of Unison was the method of choice to end it all one night, but his inner spirit prompted him to go to the Book of Proverbs instead. He read all thirty-one verses, and the passages that rang truth to him the most were in Proverbs 5:3-10:

For the lips of an immoral woman are as sweet as honey, and her mouth is smoother than oil.

But in the end, she is as bitter as poison, as dangerous as a double-edged sword.

Her feet go down to death; her steps lead straight to the grave.

For she cares nothing about the path to life. She staggers down a crooked trail and doesn't realize it.

So now, my sons, listen to me. Never stray from what I am about to say:

Stay away from her! Don't go near the door of her house!

If you do, you will lose your honor and will lose to merciless people all you have achieved.

Strangers will consume your wealth, and someone else will enjoy the fruit of your labor.

Reading the Book of Proverbs proved to be the lifeline that gave him the strength to press on in the midst of chaos. However, he chose to be intoxicated every day of the week to deal with his pain as a substitute for taking his own life, instead of turning his life over to God.

He put his beer to his lips and tilted his head back at an almost ninety-degree angle before slamming the bottle on the countertop of the bar.

"Can I get another double shot of whiskey?" Mitch asked the bartender.

"Coming right up," the bartender said.

"Hard day at work?" a beautiful young lady who was sitting next to him asked.

"I wouldn't call it a hard day at work because I no longer have a job," Mitch answered. "If I drink enough whiskey tonight, maybe I'll forget the fact that it even matters."

"Aw, I'm so sorry to hear that," she said. "I'm Natalie."

"Mitch," he said, extending his hand to her. "Nice to meet you."

The bartender brought Mitch's drinks to him, and Natalie said, "Why don't you let me get that for you?"

"What, my drinks? That's mighty kind of you, Natalie."

"Well, you are cute, and besides, you said you were between jobs."

"I'm okay...just feeling sorry for myself right now, but I'll snap out of this funk eventually."

"I'm sure you will. You just need a good woman to hold you down; that's all."

"I thought I had one, but you will always see who's really down with you when things fall apart."

"She left you with a broken heart and empty pockets, huh?"

"Not quite, but she definitely has one foot out the door."

"Well, her loss is my gain. You feel me?"

"I'm definitely feeling you, pretty lady, but I'm not that guy anymore."

"You're not that guy anymore? What the hell does that mean, Mitch?"

"I'm sorry, sweetheart. The *old* Mitch wouldn't have hesitated to jump on the opportunity to get with a fine young lady such as yourself, but I've turned over a new leaf. I can't start something new without closing the book on my present relationship."

"Wow, there are still some good men left in this world. Your girl is stupid for not recognizing that."

"I know she's messing around on me, but I can't prove it."

"Sometimes, you don't need to prove it—if a person isn't giving you what you need in a relationship, you should cut it loose."

"I agree with you, but it's not always that simple."

Mitch and Natalie continued their conversation for another hour or so, and Mitch had far surpassed the legal blood-alcohol limit. He was so inebriated that she had to literately hold him up while walking him to his car. He fell to the ground face-first in the snow when he dug in his pockets for his car keys, and she had insisted on driving him to her place, so he could sleep off his drunkenness. She owned a home in Pill Hill—a ranch-style home that she inherited from her deceased parents.

He was barely conscious when they arrived, and she helped him as he staggered to her front porch. She then covered him with a blanket after he crashed on her living room sofa, and he instantly became comatose.

"I sure can pick them," Natalie said to herself. "I hope I don't regret this in the morning."

31

Brea and Bria had just gotten back from another night of partying at a popular club on North Wells Street. Brea decided to crash at Bria's place for a little while in Oak Park, instead of going home right away. She didn't want to face Mitch to tell him that their relationship was over yet. She opted to tell him the news in the morning and deal with the drama afterwards. She still loved him, but she wasn't built to weather the storm that he was so deeply entrenched in. She thought it was best to move on and focus on her music, rather than deal with Mitch's financial problems.

She was also messing around with the new manager of her singer career, Brent Overstreet, and he had just garnered her a record deal with Strong Island Records in New York City. She had just celebrated her good news with Bria that night at the club. Her next move was to move back to New York and hit the road to promote her new album, and a relationship of any kind didn't fit into her plans.

A part of her felt responsible for Mitch's present plight, but the rest of her felt that he brought his troubles on himself. She planned on telling him the entire truth—or at least the part about her sending the pictures of them to his ex-wife. Telling Mitch about the robbery of his nightclub would not only incriminate Bria, but it would also incriminate her.

"Girl, I can't wait to fly out to New York for your listening party," Bria said. "It's gonna feel good to go back home for a while."

"I can't wait, either," Brea said. "All my dreams are about to come true."

"What are you gonna do about Mitch?" Bria asked with a smirk on her face.

"I'mma have to let that go, sis," Brea answered. "I can't let anybody hold me back, and his life is too messed up for me to do anything about it. I simply can't help him with his problems, so it's best to just end it."

"I hear you...you can't let no man keep you down. When are you gonna tell him?"

"Tomorrow. I'm going to ask him for my key back in the morning."

"Good. Get that sorry bum outta your life as soon as possible, Brea. The best way to get over your old man is to get under a new one."

"I already have that department taken care of," Brea laughed.

"What?" Bria asked. "Who is this mystery man?"

"Brent, my manager."

"Damn, you holding out on me, Brea. I guess it makes sense because you're always at the studio anyway these days."

"It's nothing serious, though—I'm just focusing on my career. We're not making any sort of commitment to each other, so he can see who he wants and so can I."

"Now that's what I'm talking about—no more falling in love with these trifling dudes. Just get you some sex and keep it moving."

"That's the plan. I'm going to turn up with as many choice guys as I possibly can because I gotta make up for lost time."

"I can't think of a reason why you shouldn't—if guys can turn up, so can girls."

Bria paused for a second to give deep thought to her next statement and said, "What if Mitch finds out about the robbery? Because we're gonna have to take him out if he does..."

"He won't, Bria," Brea answered. "And don't even think about doing something crazy like that. I still love him, so killing him is definitely out of the question."

"I'm just saying he might want some payback for breaking up with you. I don't put nothing past nobody."

"He will never find out about the club, and besides, how would he possibly tie the robbery to us?"

"Because he saw me the night Wes hired me; that's how. What if he remembers?"

"He won't. He would've said something to me by now if he remembered you, so don't worry about it."

"Okay, but if he steps to me about it, I'm gonna have to handle the situation."

Brea paused and said, "I *am* going to tell him about the pictures, though. I feel he has a right to know because I feel bad enough about leaving him..."

"Why? You don't owe him nothing, Brea. He was gonna leave his wife anyway, eventually."

"I'm going to tell him, and there's nothing you can say to change my mind. I'm going to New York with a clean slate, and I don't want what I did to him on my conscience."

"Okay, suit yourself, girl. It's your funeral."

"It'll be fine, so don't even sweat that."

"What are your plans later, that is, if Mitch doesn't kill you?"

"You are too funny, Bria. I don't have any definite plans, but I need to start packing my stuff because I'm leaving next week."

"I'm really gonna miss you once you're gone, girl."

"You should come with me. There's nothing keeping you here, is there?"

"Nah and going home would be a nice change. Give me a few months to sell or rent out my house, and I'll be there."

"Good, I'm gonna need people around me that I can trust because the music business will chew you up and spit you out."

"No doubt, and I got your back."

32

Max and his wife Jill had settled in Baton Rouge, Louisiana near the Southern University campus. They bought a house right off Scenic Drive, and he opened a barbershop a few blocks from campus. They had stayed with Jill's cousin Sabrina, who had a house off O'Neal Lane, for a couple of months before buying their own place. All their plans were coming to fruition, and they knew going legit was the best thing for their infant son.

Norris had opted to go in another direction—he wasn't feeling the South, so he took his cut from the nightclub robbery and remained in Chicago. Tyrone, on the other hand, followed Max to Baton Rouge and partnered with him because he was also a licensed barber by trade. Most of their clientele were Southern University students, and that was Max's vision from the start because he made a nice chunk of change cutting heads while he attended Texas Southern. He made haircuts affordable to the average broke college student—only ten bucks for a straight cut, five bucks for a shave, and twelve bucks for a cut and shave.

Max and Tyrone had decided to have a drink at Club Infiniti, a spot not far from the barbershop. There was a moderate crowd for a weeknight and going up there was a bit of a routine for them after closing up shop. It was a typical February night weather-wise in Baton Rouge—fifty-five degrees with a slight breeze. Tyrone had his eyes on a girl who frequented the club and wanted to say something to her.

"There she is by the dance floor," Max said. "Are you gonna holla at her or what?"

"Look at her, man," Tyrone said. "That girl is fine as hell. My game is kinda rusty, though."

"It ain't what you say. It's how you say it. Step to her with some confidence, Mack. I can't believe a killer like you is scared of a woman."

"And say what?"

"I don't know...be original and say what you feel from the heart, homeboy."

"Aiight, I'm going in."

Tyrone asked the bartender what the gorgeous young lady was drinking and ordered another round, and he walked toward the dance floor where she was standing with some of her friends. She smiled at him when he handed her the drink.

"Thank you," she said. "You're so sweet."

"You're very welcome," he said. "I'm Tyrone."

"Melissa," she said, shaking his hand. "Nice to meet you."

"You, too."

Tyrone paused and then said, "Look, I'm not gonna beat around the bush. I think you're the most beautiful woman in here, and I'd like to get to know you better. I hope I'm not coming on too strong."

"Well, you're kinda coming on strong, but I like that," Melissa said. "I like a guy who knows what he wants and knows how to go after it."

"I definitely know what I want, and I'mma start by asking you for a dance."

"Lead the way, handsome."

Tyrone led her to the middle of the dance floor after they placed their drinks on a nearby table, and Max had his eyes on them the whole time.

"My boy is in there," Max said to himself.

Tyrone danced with Melissa for at least five mix songs—and then the DJ put on the old school slow jam "Cry for You" by Jodeci to cool the people off. Tyrone embraced Melissa tightly as they slow grinded to the music, and he loved the smell of her hair and perfume. She had a killer body—she had legs for days, a shapely derriere, and her low-cut blouse revealed her C-Cup bosom. Her caramel skin was smooth, and her hair was long, black, and silky. He pulled away ever so slightly, so he could make eye contact with her, and then he planted a soft, sensuous kiss on her lips.

Max continued to sit at the bar and sip on his brew. He rarely fraternized with anyone at the club, and he solely used the spot to wind down from a hard day of work. He wasn't on any creeping-type stuff or anything remotely close to that because Jill was his heart, and he wasn't trying to do anything foolish to jeopardize their relationship. She had been the only stable constant in his crazy world up to that point.

Tyrone and Melissa walked back to the bar hand-and-hand, and Tyrone said, "I had a great time with you tonight, Melissa, and I hope I can take you out to dinner sometime."

"I'd like that, Tyrone," she said. "Let me program my number in your phone."

She took his phone and typed in her number, and he told her goodbye and kissed her again on the lips. Max started clapping once Tyrone walked back toward him at the bar.

"You did good, my brother," Max laughed. "I thought you were gonna propose to her, man."

"Why you clownin' me?" Tyrone asked.

"I'm just saying...let the girl breathe. She ain't going nowhere."

"You think she's feelin' me, huh?"

"Yeah, she's definitely feelin' you, bruh. I think you got a winner there."

"Do you think I should call her tonight?"

"Nah, wait until tomorrow. Calling her tonight makes you look desperate, but if you don't call by tomorrow, it makes you look like too much of a playa."

"Aiight, thanks for the advice. Well, I'm out. See you at the shop tomorrow."

"Aiight, peace."

Tyrone left, and Max continued to sit at the bar and work on finishing his last beer. That's when he noticed a group of wannabee tough guys circling the perimeter of the club, and he had his heat on him just in case one of those fools decided to kick something off. He also recognized one of the guys from campus—his name was Piru—a fake gangster from Compton, California. He had two other flunkies with him, named Spider and Bam, and they were known for starting trouble all around town.

Piru's trademark was robbing people he caught slipping with his AKC nine-inch special. Max was going to stop his clock right then and there if Piru had decided to bring a knife to a gunfight—they had a minor altercation at the barbershop when Piru tried to short one of his barbers for a straight cut and a shave. They settled the beef peacefully, but Max never forgot about it.

Piru locked in on Max and looked for any hint of fear, but Max met Piru's menacing glance with the cold stare of a killer. Piru simply nodded at Max and kept moving once he realized he couldn't intimidate him. Max didn't blink or flinch while gulping the last of his beer, and he didn't take his eyes off Piru or his cronies. The three of them started talking to a group of girls, whom they appeared to know, so Max tipped the bartender and ducked out of the club. He didn't want to get caught up in some mess and wanted to continue keeping a low profile—a promise he made to Jill.

33

It was a frigid Wednesday morning in Chicago, and Mitch had awakened to the smell of coffee with the usual splitting headache and upset stomach after a night of alcohol binging. He didn't recognize his surroundings and didn't remember much past drinking himself to a stupor while conversing with Natalie about his problems at the bar. It was his umpteenth hangover in as many days—he had drowned his sorrows with liquor ever since he suspected that Brea was cheating on him.

He realized he had slept with his clothes on and reached in his pockets for his car keys and cigarettes. He got up from the sofa in the living room and let the aroma lead him to the kitchen. Natalie was sitting at the kitchen table, drinking coffee and reading the paper.

"Good morning," Natalie said.

"Hey," Mitch said with a raspy throat. "How did I get here?"

"You were too drunk to drive home, and I couldn't let you go out like that."

"I really appreciate what you did for me because you don't know me from Adam."

"You're right, but I have a good feeling about you. I don't think you're the type of guy who would intentionally hurt anybody."

"That may be, but I'm sure your mother warned you about inviting strangers into your home."

"My parents are dead, and yes, they *did* raise me to have common sense. However, they also taught me to help people when they're in need."

"Well, thank you, Natalie, and I'm sorry about your parents."

"It's okay. My dad died of lung cancer ten years ago while I was away at school, and my mom died three years ago from a stroke and falling down a flight of stairs. I'm all alone now because I don't have any brothers or sisters. Are your parents still alive?"

"My mother is alive and well—I was raised by her and my grandmother. I never knew my father, though."

"I see. Cherish them while they're still here because tomorrow isn't promised."

"I know. My cousin was murdered eight months ago. He was like my brother, and I still have dreams about him being with me."

"I'm so sorry, Mitch. Did the police ever catch who did it?"

"Nah, I'm afraid not. I won't fully be able to sleep at night until I have some closure."

Natalie motioned to fill her cup with some more Taster's Choice and said, "Want some?"

"Yes, please. I need something for this hangover."

"You know, you were really throwing them back last night, and I'm surprised you even remember my name."

"I try not to drink so much that I blackout, and besides, I could never forget the name of a girl as fine as you."

"I flattered, but I'm not falling for that, *Prince Charming*. What is it with you guys, anyway? Why is it that you all are never satisfied with one woman?"

"I can't speak for all guys, Natalie, but I will say women make it too easy for guys like me."

"Guys like you? What do you mean by that?"

"It means women don't offer much resistance to successful, powerful men. Even when I was in undergrad, being part of a frat and playing basketball for the university drew in women. It's like in nature—a filly will always be drawn to the strongest stallion in the group—the alpha male if you will."

"That may apply to some women, but not all of us are like that. I was in a committed relationship for five years with a very nice guy or so I thought. He wasn't an alpha male, but we broke up because he just wasn't ready to get married."

"Why? Did you catch him cheating?"

"Yes, he cheated on me. The point I'm trying to make is that no type of guy is a sure thing. I picked a nice guy, and he still played me."

"Maybe he played you because he knew you were just settling for him—maybe he knew that he was your second or third choice. No guy wants to feel like a woman is doing him a favor by being with him—like she chose him because she felt like he should be more than happy to date her."

"That's not true, Mitch. I loved him with all my heart, but it wasn't enough. You men get bored with us as soon as you see something new and throw us away like an old pair of shoes."

"I can't argue with you there. I used to do the exact same thing, but karma catches up with everyone eventually. Now, I'm getting exactly what I deserve."

"Maybe you are to a degree, but I don't think you deserve everything Brea is doing to you. You gave her unconditional love, but she didn't give it back. She started looking for a sweeter deal the moment things started going sour for you."

Natalie leaned over and kissed Mitch on the cheek and said, "I really like you, Mitch. Forget about her and get back to having some fun in your life again. Let me help take away some of your pain—no strings attached."

Mitch smiled and said, "Your offer sounds very tempting, but I'd be no good to you or anybody else for that matter. I really like you, too, but all I can give you is friendship."

"Whoa, what kind of girl do you think I am? I just wanted to take things slow and see what happens; that's all."

"I'm sorry. I wasn't trying to imply anything. It's 2018, so it's okay for women to go after what they want."

"Well, I'm an old-fashioned girl, and like you, friendship is all that I'm offering. If it's meant to be between you and me, our friendship will blossom into something more."

"Wait a minute—you pushed up on me first—you made the first move. What's up with this old-fashioned girl stuff?"

"Yes, I did make the first move because I wanted to eliminate any uncertainty that I was interested in you. There's nothing wrong with a woman letting a man know what she wants and how she feels without trying to sleep with him."

"I hear you, and I respect your honesty, Natalie."

"Yes, I am a straight-shooter. I promise you that the more you get to know me, the more you'll love me."

"I think I like the sound of that."

They both stood up and gave each other a warm embrace. Mitch pulled away and looked into Natalie's eyes—she was almost as tall as he was—she had a five-foot-eleven slim but curvy frame—and he hadn't noticed how beautiful her hazel eyes were until that moment. She also had soft facial features—a small nose and high cheekbones like a fashion model. Her lips were full and sensual looking, and her ebony hair was short and sassy like the singer Toni Braxton's hair. Her golden-brown skin was radiant, and her fingers were long and slender like a jazz pianist. Natalie was like a Picasso painting that should be handled with care, and Mitch fully understood that fact.

"Don't you have to be at work or something?" he asked.

"No, I'm my own boss," she answered. "I do people's taxes, and I have several businesses as clients. And I'm a caterer if you're having a party anytime soon and need some good food. I usually do one event per month."

"Wow, that's dope. I was just like you before all my problems started. I used to be a financial analyst, and I owned a nightclub before the IRS seized it. I got fired once my company learned I was being audited for tax fraud. Hell, if I had hired you to do my taxes, I wouldn't be in the mess I'm in."

"You know, there just might be a silver lining in all of this, so keep your head up, sweetie."

"I hear what you're saying, but it still feels like the weight of the world is on my shoulders."

"I can help you through all of this if you'll let me."

"Okay then, you can start by helping me find my car keys and cigarettes. I think I lost them last night."

"Yeah, you almost did—I picked up your keys for you when you dropped them on the ground after falling on your face. As for your cigarettes, I can't help you there. You really should quit, anyway."

"You're right. Maybe I will."

Mitch paused briefly and said, "Can you take me back to the bar to get my car?"

"Sure, give me a few minutes to get dressed."

Natalie went to her bedroom to change, and they left about five minutes later. The bar was ten minutes away, and Mitch's car was parked right in front of the club still intact. He had downgraded from his Benz to a used Honda Accord.

"Thanks for dropping me off," Mitch said. "Here's my card. Call me anytime."

"Not until you call me first," Natalie said. "Here's *my* card—a gentleman is supposed to pursue the lady, not the other way around, right?"

"Right. I'll try to remember that. Take care."

"Yes, you should. Bye, Mitch."

Natalie waved at him as she drove off, and Mitch unlocked his car and got in it. Natalie's comment about being a gentleman made him laugh out loud to himself. She was a bit of a tease in his opinion, and he felt deep down that their relationship was probably not going to blossom into much more than friendship. He also felt he had outgrown what she was offering him—her sweetness, her kindness, and her refreshing honesty were things his corrupted mind needed but didn't desire. Brea had him so jacked up mentally that he actually thought he was taking a step backwards by entertaining the thought of a relationship with Natalie. Nobody could possibly make me feel the way Brea does, he thought. What a damn fool.

He looked at the card she gave him—Natalie Barnes, Certified Public Accountant. Impressive. She keeps people's books all year-round and caters food on the side. And she's beautiful. Damn, why is she still single? Because guys like me don't have their stuff together; that's why.

His cell phone rang right before he was about to drive off.

"Hello," Mitch said.

"Hi, Mitch, this is Detective Grimes," he said. "I'm going to need you to come down to the station to answer some questions about the robbery of your nightclub and the murder of your cousin."

"Is there a break in the case?"

"Yes, but I'd like to discuss it with you in person."

"Okay, I'll be there in about an hour."

Mitch disconnected the call and continued to sit in the car. Who did they catch? Was he one of the shooters? Questions incessantly swirled in his mind and made his heart race. He finally started his car and headed west down 111th Street en route to the Bridgeview Police Department.

34

Brea wiped some sweat from her forehead while she worked out to a Shaun T video. She had gained about fifteen pounds over the past year, so she wanted to tone up her body for her upcoming video shoot. Her debut album was about to drop in a few weeks, and she planned on hitting the ground running with her first single getting that BET rotation.

She left Bria's place earlier that morning as soon as the sun had risen because she wanted to get a jumpstart on her day. She was about ten minutes into her workout when there was a knock at her door. She paused the DVD and looked through the peephole to see who it was.

"What are you doing here, Brent?" Brea asked. "Mitch is subject to pop up at any moment."

"Just open the door, Brea," Brent answered. "I've got some good news."

"Couldn't you have told me over the phone?" Brea asked as she opened the door.

"No, this kind of news deserves to be delivered in person," Brent answered.

"Well, what is it?"

"The record label wants to shoot the video tomorrow. How fast can you book a flight to New York?"

"For real? Damn, that's awesome, Brent. I'll get on it right now."

"Great, because your video is slated to be on BET and MTV in the next few weeks, so get ready."

"I was born ready, sweetheart."

Brent grabbed Brea by the waist and started kissing her ferociously. She matched his intensity with some ferociousness of her own and tackled him on her sofa. He didn't mind the sweat from her workout—it turned him on even more, in fact. It didn't take long for them to rip off each other's clothes and partake in a morning romp. Brea got the workout she had hoped to get and then some.

Brent was just as sweaty as she was as they cuddled naked on her sofa.

"I can't get enough of you, Brea," he said. "By the way, I got us a temporary place in downtown Manhattan."

"That's nice, baby," she said. "I'll start looking for my own spot once we wrap up our first tour, and I can keep most of my stuff in storage."

"What's the rush? You can stay with me as long as you want, you know. I don't want you to leave..."

"You're my manager, Brent, not my man."

"But..."

"No buts. Business is business, and if we have a little fun on the side, so be it. But that's as far as it goes."

"It's Mitch, isn't it?"

"No, Mitch has nothing to do with it. Mitch and I are about to be over."

"That's good to know."

"Look, I appreciate you sharing the good news with me and giving me a great morning workout, but you have to go."

"I know. Call me later, okay? Just to let me know you booked your flight."

"Okay, I'll talk to you later on tonight."

He got dressed, kissed her on the lips, and left. She then grabbed her workout clothes and tossed them in her clothing hamper before going to the bathroom to shower. She was determined to keep Brent at bay and not let things get out of hand. Easier said than done, though.

35

Max rolled over, still asleep, and pressed against Jill's soft and shapely bottom. It wasn't quite ten o'clock yet, and Max wasn't due at the shop until twelve. Jill had gotten up a couple of hours ago to change and feed Gary Jr., and she had gotten back in the bed to lie down once the baby fell asleep again. She decided to give him something memorable to start the day. He moaned and groaned before awakening to his morning treat, and she was totally engrossed in pleasing her man until he was completely satisfied. He sighed while she laid her head on his chest, and he gently stroked her French braids as he held her in his arms.

Even though she was a little rough around the edges with the Timberland boots and large bamboo hoop earrings, she was a sweetheart underneath her tough exterior. Her copper-tone skin was smooth and silky, her five-foot-four-inch frame was shapely and sexy, and her beautiful brown eyes were ever so inviting. As a former women's basketball player at TSU, one of her top priorities was keeping in shape.

"I love you, baby," Jill said. "I hope you liked my surprise."

"I loved it, boo," Max said. "You really know how to treat a brutha like a king."

"Yes, I do, and you are my king."

Max paused and said, "What you got going on today?"

"I'mma do some grocery shopping after I get my nails done. Why?"

"I wanted to take you and Junior out to dinner later. The shop is doing real good, and I wanna celebrate."

"That's great, baby. Where are we going?"

"I was thinking we could go to Deanie's in New Orleans. Their seafood is off the chain."

"That's a good idea, Gary. What time do you get off?"

"I'mma try to get off around five, and Mack is gonna close up shop for me."

"Okay, I'll be ready, but I don't want Junior out around all those people yet. He's just getting over his cold, and I don't want him to get sick again."

"That's cool, maybe your cousin Sabrina can keep him."

"Yeah, I'll give her a call right now."

Jill reached over the bed to grab the phone to call Sabrina, and Max went to the bathroom to take a shower.

"Hey, girl," Jill said.

"Hey, cuz," Sabrina said. "What's up?"

"Can you watch Junior tonight for a few hours? Me and Gary are going out to celebrate."

"Sure, girl, I can watch him. What y'all celebrating?"

"His barbershop is doing real good, and he wants to take me out to dinner."

"That's great, Jill—you have a good man. Junior will be in good hands, so y'all have fun, okay?"

"Thanks, I owe you."

"Don't worry about it...you're family. Bye."

"Bye."

Jill got up to fix breakfast once she ended her call, and Max was dressed and ready for work in fifteen minutes. He came into the kitchen once he smelled the food cooking.

"Your breakfast will be ready in a minute, Gary," Jill said.

"Okay, I'mma go in the living room to watch some t.v."

She brought him his plate and a glass of orange juice a few minutes later.

"Sabrina said she can watch Junior," Jill said.

"Cool," Max said. "Where are you getting your nails done at?"

"It's this new shop right off Plank Road that just opened up. This girl I met at the mall told me they do a good job, so I'm gonna give them a try."

"Be careful—I heard some dudes over there like to stick people up."

"Don't worry, baby. I'll keep my guard up."

Max finished his food and took his plate and glass to the kitchen. He kissed Jill goodbye and said, "I've gotta pick up some supplies for the shop, so I'mma head on out."

"Alright, see you later," she said.

36

Mitch arrived at the police station and was greeted by a stoic officer at the front desk. The officer sounded like someone had urinated in her morning coffee when she told Mitch to have a seat until Detective Grimes was ready to see him.

Mitch reflected on his relationship with Brea while he waited for Grimes. It was two days before Valentine's Day, and he was torn between giving her the engagement ring that he had bought her and taking it back to the jeweler. She had proven that she wasn't worth the trouble, or at least that's what his mind told him. His heart, on the other hand, told him to make a complete fool of himself in order to win back Brea's love and affection. He also thought about Wesley—he asked himself what he would do in a situation like this.

His daydream was interrupted once Grimes tapped him on the shoulder.

"Follow me to my office," Detective Grimes said.

Grimes led Mitch down the corridor to his office that was on the right-hand side of the hallway. Mitch had a seat in the chair facing Grimes at his desk.

"What did you find?" Mitch said.

"We have a suspect in custody, and that's why I called you in," Detective Grimes answered. "I need you to look at a lineup to see if you recognize this person, or maybe you remember seeing her face at the club one night before the robbery."

"The suspect is a woman?"

"Yes, sir, an informant of ours knew something about the robbery, and in exchange for her freedom, she gave this woman up."

"What was your informant charged with?"

"She was an exotic dancer facing prostitution charges. Come on. Let's find out if this is the person we're looking for."

Grimes and Mitch went to a room where the five suspects were standing in a lineup behind a surveillance mirror. Another detective was present in the room when they arrived.

"This is Detective Martin," Detective Grimes said.

Mitch shook Martin's hand and said, "I recognize one of the women. Her name is Bria Jones, my girlfriend's twin sister."

"Are you sure about this?" Detective Grimes asked.

"I'm one hundred percent positive, sir," Mitch answered.

"We suspect she was the one who planted the guns in your club on the night in question," Detective Grimes said.

Mitch took a moment to soak everything in—then he suddenly remembered the night Wesley hired the last two dancers at the club, and one of the girls was Bria. He didn't get a good look at her face because she was leaving with the other girl as he was coming in—she looked different back then because she didn't have braids that night. That was the only time he ever saw her at the club, and that's why he didn't remember her at first.

"Did she name anyone else in the robbery?" Mitch asked.

"I'm sorry, but she maintains her innocence and won't bulge," Detective Martin said. "Her arraignment is later today."

"Damn, I really need to know who else was involved, so I can put this behind me," Mitch said.

"Don't worry, Mitch. We will get to the bottom of this," Detective Grimes said. "I appreciate your cooperation, and we will contact you once we have something new."

"Thank you, Detective Grimes," Mitch said.

Mitch left the precinct stunned. The Jones twins had pulled the wool over his eyes, and he wanted answers. He figured out that Brea conveniently caught a flat tire the night she called him, so he wouldn't be at the club when it got robbed. He also came to the conclusion that Brea probably sent the photos of the two of them to his ex-wife Sandra.

He headed straight to Brea's place to find out the entire truth and arrived an hour or so later. Traffic was thick, and it frustrated him to the point of an almost total meltdown.

"Get the hell outta the way, stupid!" Mitch shouted at the motorist in front of him.

The guy was driving slowly in the left-hand lane on Interstate 94, and there was nobody in front of him for at least a hundred yards.

This drove Mitch insane as he practically rode on the guy's bumper. The guy seemed to drive even slower just to piss him off.

"Get this piece of junk outta my damn way!" he shouted. "Some of us have somewhere to be!"

This continued for about a mile before Mitch was able to get around him in the middle lane. Mitch angrily glanced over at the driver before speeding off. He finally arrived at Brea's after fighting through more traffic and giving another motorist the bird on the expressway. He parked next to her black Mustang and got out. He then let himself in and noticed boxes on the floor. The sight of it enraged him even more.

"Brea!" he boomed. "What the hell is going on?!"

"Keep your voice down, Mitch," Brea said, emerging from her bedroom wearing a bra and panties. "You're gonna disturb my neighbors."

"Screw your neighbors, Brea. You lied to me, dammit!"

"What the hell are you talking about, Mitch? You're crazy."

"No, you and Bria set me up, and now my cousin is dead because of you!"

"Who told you that?"

"Who do you think? I just picked your stupid sister out of a lineup at the Bridgeview Police Department. I know she was the one who planted the guns in my club, and I know that you knew about it. How could you do this to me, Brea?"

"I'm so sorry, baby—I never meant for any of this to happen."

"Just tell me the truth!"

"I—Bria asked me to stake out your club and find out who the owners were. I didn't know they were gonna rob you all until it was almost too late, and that's when I made up the lie about catching a flat tire. If I didn't, you'd be dead."

"Don't try to turn this around on me—who else robbed my damn club?"

"I don't know, Mitch. I swear!"

"You really expect me to believe that?"

"I swear I don't know, Mitch—I didn't have anything to do with it."

"Your sister is facing prison, so I suggest you come clean, Brea."

"Bria lied to me about her true intentions at first. She claimed she wanted me to study how your club was run, so she could open up her own spot. She told me she wanted to steal some of your ideas."

"That's not all she stole..."

"Look, Mitch, what's done is done. I can't change what happened to your cousin."

"Then tell me why you sent those pictures of us to my ex-wife? I never would've done to you what you did to me."

"I wanted you all to myself, and besides, you were gonna leave her anyway."

"Not your call to make, Brea. You have some nerve—you messed up my life, and now you're packing your stuff and leaving me!"

"Wrong, you ruined your life, not me."

"Are you leaving me?"

"Yes, I'm leaving Chicago, and yes, I'm breaking up with you. Your problems are too much for me to handle. I'm trying to get my music career off, and I don't have time to babysit you, Mitch."

"Hold up, Brea, I never asked you for anything—the only thing I ever wanted to do was love you and take care of you. My whole existence centered on making you happy from the moment I met you, but that still wasn't enough."

"Who are you kidding, Mitch? You can't even take care of yourself, so how are you gonna take care of me? Please, you drive a used Honda Accord, so what makes you think you can afford me?"

"So, this is what it all comes down to, huh? Some damn money? I thought we were better than that."

"I told you how it was gonna be from jump street. You still gotta pay to play, sweetheart."

"You used me, and you played me for a damn fool. You don't care about anybody but yourself."

"I never meant to hurt you, and for the record, I *do* love you."

"Save it, Brea. You know, deep down I always knew it would come to this, but I dove in headfirst anyway. It's a shame too because, even after all that has happened, you still can't be totally honest with me."

"Be honest about what? I told you everything."

"Nah, not everything. What's up with the open condom wrapper on the floor?"

"Okay, Mitch, I'm sleeping with someone else. Is that what you want to hear?"

"I just want to hear the truth."

"What difference does it make?"

"You're real sloppy. You could've at least kept it real with me."

"You're right. I should've been honest with you, but like I said, I didn't want to hurt you."

"I'm a big boy, and I can handle it. Here's your key, Brea. Have a nice life."

He tossed her key on her living room table and walked out. She couldn't look him in the eye after he had spoken his piece and simply hung her head in shame. He tried his best to fight back tears from the heartbreak of losing the girl of his dreams, but he couldn't hold it together any longer. He managed to keep his composure and not fall apart in front of her, but he let out his emotions as soon as he got inside his car. He sobbed for several minutes before he dug in his pocket and pulled out Brea's engagement ring. He then threw it on the floor on the passenger's side of his car in anger before he drove off.

He was determined to find out what happened, so he decided to pay Cedric Nash a visit. He felt that Cedric was holding something back the last time they had spoken, and it was high time he found out what that *something* was.

37

Tommy G had set up shop near the Southern University campus. The rent per month for the house that he stayed in was dirt cheap, and a good portion of his clientele was his coworkers and their friends. He also had a large number of students from Southern, and he had several people from a few of the local bars that he frequented. Weed was his drug of choice to sell, and he was able to maintain a low profile, even though he moved a significant amount of weight. He sold enough weed to stash away a good chunk of change for a rainy day and had a full-time job as a cashier at a Chevron gas station. The gig was merely a cover to hide the fact that he was still hustling.

It was his day off, so he cracked open a forty-ounce of Old English malt liquor to start his afternoon. There was a knock at the door a few seconds later, and he figured it was a student looking to cop some weed.

"What's happenin', Tommy," Piru said, giving him some dap.

"It's all good, my brother," Tommy G said. "What you need?"

"Lemme get a twenty sack."

"I got you."

Tommy G went to his bedroom, while Piru waited in the living room. The house smelled like incense—masking the odor of the fresh marijuana he had stashed in the house. His television was on, and there was a rerun of a college basketball game on ESPN.

He came back to the living room with a Ziploc bag of product, and Piru handed him a twenty-dollar bill.

"You got the best weed in town, homeboy," Piru said. "Where you get your stash?"

"That's classified information, Piru," Tommy G answered. "Why, you looking to get put on?"

"Hell yeah, man. I'm tired of robbing these suckas, yo. I'm down if you wanna expand your business."

"I'm trying to keep what I do on the low. You feel me?"

"Yeah, I hear you, Tommy, but a brutha gotta eat, too."

Tommy G rubbed his chin and said, "Alright, here's what I'm gonna do. I'mma front you some product today, and I want a fifty percent cut of what you sell on the Friday after next."

"That's fair, homeboy...good lookin' out."

"If you get busted, you don't know me. Understood?"

"I got you, Tommy."

Tommy G went back to his bedroom and came out with about a pound of weed. Piru's eyes and gold-tooth grin widened when he handed him the package.

"Thanks for putting me on, Tommy," Piru said. "You won't be sorry."

"Um hum," Tommy said. "That's roughly about two grand worth of product I'm fronting you, Piru. See you in about a week."

"I can handle it," Piru said. "You won't regret this, man."

Piru left Tommy G's house looking like he had just won the lottery, and Tommy G sat down on his sofa in deep thought. Not the move he had planned on making, he thought. Piru was a loyal repeat customer, but he really didn't want him on his payroll. However, he figured it was better to put Piru on than have to watch his back for the potential threat of him robbing him for his stash. Piru and his crew were known for robbing people all around town, and he didn't want to draw any unwanted attention to himself by killing any one of them.

"That dude has one time to cross me, and it's lights out," Tommy G said to himself.

He then picked up his phone and called his friend from work.

"What's up, Ronnie?" Tommy G asked.

"Nothing much," Ronnie replied. "What you got going on?"

"It's time to expand our operation."

"Word? What you got planned?"

"I added another guy on the payroll—he's gonna bring me some more of that Southern U clientele, you feel me?"

"Yeah, that's sounds like a good idea. What's this dude's name?"

"His name is Piru, and you might have heard of him. He's a career student...been down here seven years and only got about sixty credit hours."

"Yeah, I know that fool...a wannabee gangsta from Compton. This lunatic is gonna get himself killed one day."

"Yeah, but he's trying to up his street game."

"You trust him?"

"Yeah, I trust him enough. He's hungry, so I'mma see what he's made of."

"Oh, okay. If this dude tries to cross us, I'mma lullaby him and his posse."

"I'm one step ahead of you, my brother. I doubt if he'll bite the hand that feeds him, though."

"You can't be too careful, Tommy."

"I know. Talk to you later."

"Alright, later."

Tommy G hung up the phone and took a swig of his beer. It was eight months later, and his drug operation was now about to be one hundred percent functional again. Certainly not the kind of light he wanted to shine on his business. His uncle Cedric warned him to stay out of the spotlight, but the spotlight found him instead.

38

Norris Adams made a mint flipping his first property that he bought for next to nothing—a foreclosed HUD house in the far south suburbs. He no longer had to lie about what he did for a living in order to attract women because now he was actually doing it. He could never afford the down payment on a property until he had pulled off that last robbery with Max, Tyrone, and his deceased brother Quentin.

Norris bought the house for twenty grand, and he pumped forty more into the house before selling it for a cool one hundred fifty grand. He was living the life that he always wanted, and being a licensed carpenter never felt better. Norris was able to go legit, and he was able to enjoy the fruits of his labor.

Norris heard a growl in the pit of his stomach, and he was a few blocks from Del Frisco's, an upscale restaurant off North Michigan Avenue. His new fling, Kia Black, was meeting him there for a lunch date. They had been seeing each other for about two months, and they had met at Club Ecstasy the night it got robbed the previous summer. She worked a mile from the restaurant at a firm on Wacker Drive as an associate attorney.

He circled the perimeter once and found a space a half-block from the restaurant. His ivory-colored Nissan Maxima sparkled from the fresh hand wash and coat of Armor All on the tires. He made sure his twenty-inch chrome rims weren't too close to the curb before finally squeezing into the space barely big enough to house his car. He then checked with the hostess inside the restaurant only to discover that Kia had already gotten them a booth near the back of the restaurant. She was looking at her watch when he got to the table.

"You're five minutes late," Kia scolded him. "I have to be back at two."

"It was hard finding parking, baby," he said, trying to soften her mood. "Did you order our food?"

"What do you think?"

"Why are you being so nasty?"

"Because you don't respect my time, Norris. If you want to continue seeing me, you'd better step up your game."

"I'm sorry, Kia. Please don't be mad."

"I'm not mad—I'm just under a lot of pressure at work, and my boss isn't giving me much room to breathe."

"Things will get better, I promise."

"And how the hell do you know that? Please don't say stupid stuff like that because you're not helping me."

"You don't have to jump down my throat. I was just trying to make you feel better."

"You're not God—you can't make my pain go away with these worn-out clichés that pop up into your tiny little brain. Sometimes, I just want you to listen...to empathize with me without trying to solve my problems."

They sat in silence after her diatribe until the food came a few minutes later. Norris stared off in the direction of other patrons enjoying their lunch while Kia continued to look at some notes from work. He lightly tapped his fingers on the table for a brief instance, but her cold stare caused him to stop his nervous fidgeting abruptly. Kia was the type of woman who's always ready to debate someone—practicing law as a profession was a natural choice that accentuated her combative natural.

The server finally brought out a plate of salmon and rice with asparagus tips for Norris, and a Caesar salad for Kia. Norris frowned when the server placed his plate on the table.

"Careful because it's hot," the server said to Norris.

"What the hell is this?" Norris asked.

"Would you lower your voice," Kia urged. "I swear I can't take you anywhere."

"Let me know if you all need anything else," the server said before she quickly walked away from their table.

"I'm starting to get real tired of you always tryin' to boss me around, Kia—you-are-not my damn mother!"

"Calm down, Norris, please..."

"I told you I don't like seafood. Stop treating me like I'm your damn son!"

"Okay...okay, baby. I'm sorry."

"I go outta my way to try to please you, but all you do is piss on me. You're fine as hell, but I can't take your attitude anymore."

The manager of the restaurant overheard Norris shouting and came over to their table and said, "Is everything all right over here? I can't have you two distributing my other guests like this."

Norris pulled a hundred dollar bill out of his pocket and placed it on the table. He looked the manager in the eye and replied, "Everything's cool. Sorry for the disturbance, sir."

Norris grabbed his coat and car keys and left the restaurant. Kia ran out after him and stopped him halfway down the block. She broke one of her heels and ripped the ruined heel off of her shoe in disgust after grabbing his right arm. He snatched his arm away and turned to face her. The cold wind blew her long, jet-black hair in her face, and she struggled to keep it out of her eyes.

"What do you want?" Norris asked.

"I'm sorry, Norris," she answered. "Please don't go."

"You're too deep for me, baby girl. I'm done with this relationship."

"You're breaking up with me?"

"Yeah, I can't do this anymore. I really like you, Kia, but you're crazy. One minute you're the sweetest girl in the world, and the next you're chewing me out for no reason. I can't function like that..."

"I don't want things to end like this, sweetheart. It's just I've been hurt so many times before that I don't know how to trust a guy and let things flow anymore."

"I didn't do what those other guys did to you...maybe I'm not the man for you."

"Can we just start over? We can go someplace else to eat if you want."

"Nah, that's okay...I lost my appetite. Don't you have to be back at work?"

"Forget work, baby. You're what matters to me right now. I never had a guy treat me the way that you do, and it scares the hell out of me. I act the way that I do because I don't want to get dogged out again..."

"That's not fair, Kia, because I never played any games from day one. I changed my whole life just to be with you, but all you do is try to control me."

"Huh? You changed your life for me?"

"Yeah, I've done some pretty twisted stuff in my past, but I turned my life around after I met you."

"What kind of twisted stuff, Norris?"

"I was a criminal, Kia. I sold drugs for a while, and at one point, I even started robbing drug dealers."

She covered her mouth with her hand before saying, "Did you ever kill anyone?"

He paused and said, "Yes, I've killed people. I'm not proud of it, but I did it. You can't turn me into this idea of man that you have in your head, and I realize now that I'm not the guy you are looking for."

"Why did you wait until today to tell me this? I grew up with criminals like you in my family, and I never would've let things get this far if you just would've leveled with me."

"I never lied to you. It just never came up..."

"Never came up? You had more than enough time to tell me."

"Tell you what? That I used to be a drug dealer and a killer? That's not just something you reveal to somebody over dinner or walk on the beach."

"I'm not just somebody, Norris. I had a right to know who you really were and to choose whether or not I wanted to get involved with you. You took that choice away from me."

"It is what it is, Kia. You asked me what was up, and I told you the truth. I'm sorry for messing up your life by not telling you sooner."

"I don't know if I can get past this, Norris. You've killed people..."

"I'm not asking you to get past it. What I did was all part of the game, and I can't change that."

"Well, I guess this is goodbye."

"I'm afraid it is. Goodbye, Kia."

He hopped in his car that was parked a few yards away and wasted no time driving off once the busy traffic subsided. She continued to stand outside briefly as she watched his car disappear down Oak Street, and a tear slowly streamed down her face and fell to the ground. The chocolate beauty who could've easily modeled for Vogue limped back to the entrance of the restaurant as the salt and melting snow crunched beneath her shoes, and she quickly went back inside to warm up.

She still had a little time left on her lunch break, and surprisingly, the wait staff didn't clear their table yet. She got her salad to go and paid the waitress with the cash that Norris left on the table and exited the front entrance once her Uber driver arrived.

39

Mitch drove around for a couple of hours trying to locate Cedric but came up empty. Cedric owned a variety of businesses that hid his drug money, like a chain of liquor stores, various rental properties, an auto repair shop, and a carwash to name a few, and Mitch was going to try his luck stopping by Cedric's liquor store right off the Dan Ryan Expressway on 87th Street.

Cedric was like family to Mitch because Cedric moved up the ranks in the drug business that Mitch's uncle ran many years ago. Mitch opted to go to college rather than join the *family business*—a move that Cedric repeatedly urged him to do.

Mitch parked his car in the strip mall on the south side of 87th Street and went inside the store. He asked the cashier if Cedric was there, and Cedric came out of his office to greet Mitch once he heard his voice.

"What's up, Mitch?" Cedric asked. "What brings you by here?"

"Mr. Nash," Mitch said, ignoring Cedric's question, "you're hard man to find. Looking good, I might add."

"You're not, Mitch. How the hell did you let yourself go like this?"

"What, you don't like the scruffy look?"

"Nah, man, you could really use a shave. So, what brings you by? I know this ain't a social visit."

"You were right."

"Right about what?"

"Brea. She played me for a fool. She was messing around with another dude behind my back."

"Let's go into my office."

Mitch followed Cedric inside his cramped little space in the back of the store, and Cedric shut the door behind them and said, "I'm sorry to hear that, little brother. I tried to warn you, though, but I guess you had to see it for yourself. If you need anything, I'm here for you."

"As a matter of fact, I do need something from you."

"Sure, name it."

"I need to know everything you know about Wes's murder. I could sense you were holding something back from me the last time we talked."

"Leave it alone, Mitch. The streets ain't for you..."

"Yeah, yeah...you've given me that speech a thousand times."

"You're smart, Mitch, and unlike the rest of us, you had options. I promised your uncle George that I'd make sure you stayed clear of the drug game before he got locked up."

"And I really appreciate that, Ced, but I'm not a kid anymore. I need to find out what happened to my cousin, and I won't rest until I do."

"You have too much to lose, bro, so no, I can't help you."

"Look at me, man—I've hit rock bottom. The IRS seized my club and my house, and I got fired from my job. I'm also one step away from prison, so you see, I don't have a damn thing to lose."

"Okay, Mitch, I'll tell you what I know. Do you remember when my spot got knocked last summer?"

"Yeah, five of your guys got murdered, but your nephew escaped, right?"

"That's right, and the same guys who hit my drug house are the same guys who shot up your club."

"And how do you know this?"

"Because one of them used to work for me."

"What's his name?"

"His name is Tyrone Mack, and there were four of them altogether."

"Bria told you, didn't she? I know she had something to do with it too because the Bridgeview police have her in custody."

"Bria's in jail?"

"Yeah, but she didn't tell the police anything. They say she was the one who planted the guns in my club, but she denies the whole thing."

"Yeah, she was in on it with them, but they shorted her on her cut."

“Damn, there’s no honor among thieves. I was thinking there’s still a good chance that she might walk because it’s her word against some prostitute’s.”

“She’s gonna need a good lawyer, though.”

“Let me ask you this—if you know who hit your spot, why haven’t you gone after them?”

“I did—I mean I had all of them on my radar, but one of them had the drop on me and my family. I had to let them go, and nobody has seen them since.”

“Who had the drop on you?”

“This dude they call Max. He was the leader of the crew.”

“Who, Gary Maxwell?”

“Yeah, and he admitted that he shot Wes. I think he was the mastermind behind the whole scheme.”

“You know this for a fact?”

“Absolutely—Big Ty and Max hit my dope house and your club, and they vanished without a trace. So, you know this guy, Max?”

“Yeah, I know him—he used to be my best friend. I swear I’m gonna kill this backstabbing lowlife. ”

“Relax, Mitch. We will figure this out together. I promise you.”

“There’s nothing to figure out, man. I’m going to hunt Max and this guy Tyrone down and put them six feet under, and that’s my word.”

“Okay, then, just make sure I’m there when you dig their graves.”

40

Jill decided to get a pedicure in addition to a manicure because the nail technician had done such a fabulous job on her hands. Good thing she had worn her Nike sandals rather than the Timberlands she was accustomed to wearing. The girl who did her nails was a junior at Southern University majoring in political science. She worked at the salon to help pay for her tuition, and she had an eight-month-old daughter to look after.

The nail tech's name was Tisha Black, and Jill hit it off with her instantly. Tisha was witty, funny, and very vivacious—she had Jill laughing the entire time with her stories about school and the father of her infant daughter.

"And this fool still can't properly change the baby's diapers," Tisha said. "I love him, but he's such a man."

"I hear you girl," Jill said. "What would they do without us, right?"

"Play with themselves and die of starvation."

"You are so crazy, Tisha."

"Hey, what are you all doing tonight? We should all go out for drinks or something."

"We can't do it tonight, but we can certainly hang out tomorrow."

"That's cool. I'll see what Jimmy has going on tomorrow night because he has a game earlier that evening."

"A game? Is he a coach?"

"Nah, he plays for Southern, and they have a really good team this year. He's their starting point guard."

"Damn, that's what's up. I used to play college basketball, too...I played for Texas Southern a few years ago."

"Yeah? You and your man should come to Jimmy's game tomorrow."

"Sure, we definitely will. Gary loves basketball."

"Did he play ball?"

"Yeah, he played his freshman year, but he got kicked off the team and out of school in the middle of our sophomore year."

"What happened?"

"It's a long story," Jill said hesitantly. "I'll tell you about it one day."

"It's okay if you're not comfortable talking about it," Tisha said reassuringly. "Nobody's perfect."

"Gary's very private, and he doesn't like to put his business out there."

"I understand."

"How much I owe you?"

"Just give me thirty...you're family now."

"I feel the same way about you, too. Thanks, girl."

"No problem. What's your number? I can program it in my phone."

Jill and Tisha exchanged numbers, and Jill handed Tisha a fifty-dollar bill.

"Keep the change, girl," Jill said. "I'll call you later tonight."

"Thanks," Tisha said, giving Jill a hug. "I should be home around nine."

"Okay, talk to you later."

Jill left the salon and motioned toward her car parked around the corner of the shop. Then suddenly, a masked man grabbed her from behind and wrestled her to the ground. He put a switchblade to her throat and shouted, "Give me all your money or else!"

"Please don't hurt me!" Jill cried. "Here's my purse...please don't hurt me!"

The masked man snatched Jill's purse from her hand, pulled out her wallet, and tossed her purse on the ground. He had his eyes on her the entire time while extracting the cash out of her wallet and dropping it in the grass near the purse. She lay frozen in terror on the pavement, and the guy sprinted down the block and disappeared on a side street. She had the notion to call the police, but she opted not to dial 911.

She then picked herself, her purse, and her wallet off the ground, got in her car, and drove around in a daze for about thirty minutes before arriving at Max's shop. She was still crying when she went inside and was uncertain about how he was going to react.

"What the hell happened?" Max asked.

"Somebody robbed me," Jill answered, and her voice was quivering.

"Huh?" Tyrone asked, taking his attention away from cutting his customer's hair. "Did you get a good look at him?"

"Yeah, did you get a good look at his face?" Max asked, rubbing her on her back.

"No, he had a mask on," Jill answered. "He threw me on the ground and put a knife to my throat..."

"Dammit!" Max boomed. "Somebody's gonna pay for this!"

"Calm down, bruh," Tyrone said. "We're gonna find out who did this to you, Jill. Do you remember what he had on?"

"I think he had on a blue t-shirt with 'I Love LA' on it and some plaid shorts," Jill answered.

"He had on a 'I Love LA' shirt, and he had a switchblade?" Max asked.

"Yes," Jill answered as she wiped the tears from her eyes. "And he was tall and skinny."

"I know who did this to you, baby," Max said. "Mack, hold down the shop until I get back—Jill, go home and wait for me."

"Where are you going, baby?" Jill asked.

"On campus to get some answers," Max replied.

"Be careful, homeboy," Tyrone urged.

"Yeah, I will," Max said.

41

The police released Bria due to the fact that she passed a polygraph test, and there was no concrete proof to connect her to the robbery or the murders at the club in any way. Her cell phone records also indicated she was home at the time of robbery and subsequent murders in Mitch's club. The exotic dancer's statement was merely deemed hearsay and possibly defamation of character. Brea came to pick her up, and they left the Bridgeview jail together.

Bria got picked up right after Brea left her house the previous night, and the detectives literally dragged her out of bed and took her directly to jail. The police wouldn't even let her make her phone call to her lawyer until the later part of the morning.

"You're really wrecking my flow, Bria," Brea said before they exited the parking lot. "I have a plane to catch in a few hours."

"And where are you going?" Bria asked.

"I have a video shoot in New York tomorrow if you must know."

"Wow, that's great, sis. You're well on your way..."

"Don't try to avoid the situation at hand, Bria. What happened here?"

"What does it look like? Some tramp from the club tried to drop the dime on me, but she ain't fading nothing over here."

"Cut the tough-girl act, all right? You're not totally out of the woods yet."

"Brea, please...that trick didn't see me do a damn thing. Hell, nobody saw me do anything; trust me. She's just trying to save herself by saying I did it because I quit dancing at the club a few days before it all went down. Besides, I passed the lie detector test."

"Trust you? Mitch knows everything, and I can't afford to lose what I worked so hard for."

"Yes, sis, trust me. Your ex can't prove a thing because he wasn't even there when everything hit the fan."

"But he knows you were in on it because he remembered your face at the club the night Wes hired you. What if Mitch tells the police what he knows, and they decide to charge you again?"

"It's not what you know; it's what you can prove, Brea. Remember that."

"Whatever you say. You're on your own with this mess—I'm leaving Chicago, and the only time I'm ever gonna grace this city with my presence again is when I have to perform here."

"Look, you're worrying about nothing. It's over, and I'm free."

"Are you hungry," Brea asked, changing the subject.

"Hell yeah," Bria answered. "They snatched me outta bed and barely let me put some clothes on before hauling me off to jail."

"Wanna go to that pancake house that's around the corner from you?"

"Nah, I gotta taste for some chicken. Let's go to Popeye's."

"You're sure? I got some time to kill before my flight tonight."

"Yeah, girl, I'm sure. I don't feel like sitting in any damn restaurant."

"Okay."

"So, did you find a place to stay yet?"

"No, not yet. I'm gonna stay with Brent until I find something."

"That's not a good idea, Brea..."

"He knows what time it is. It's only for a couple of weeks tops, and then I'm going to get my own place in Manhattan."

"I'm telling you it's a bad idea. This guy ain't gonna let you outta his sight for one second."

"Now, it's my turn to tell *you* to trust *me*."

"Whatever. You be having these dudes whipped and crazy out their minds—I bet he's gonna be stalking you for sure."

"I must say my stuff is the bomb, you know."

"Girl, you're crazy as hell. Well, when you do find your own place, make sure you have enough room for me."

"Don't worry. I got you."

42

Mitch was asking neighbors about Max's whereabouts—the first place he checked was the apartment high-rise Max and Jill rented on 71st and South Shore Drive but soon discovered they had vacated the premises. Max kept a low profile and never fraternized with anyone, so Mitch had to put the brakes on his search temporarily.

His mother and grandmother stayed in Jeffery Manor, a neighborhood on the southeast side of the city. Mitch parked in a space across the street from his grandmother's house, and he didn't recognize any of the people standing idly on the block. He did speak to a couple of guys, who appeared to be harmless, hanging out in front of the house, and they spoke back. He then used his key to unlock the door and go inside the house.

"Momma!" Mitch shouted. "Nana!"

"Mitchell, is that you?" Nana asked, peeking out of the kitchen.

"Hey, Nana," he said, giving his grandmother a warm embrace. "I've really missed you."

"How are you, baby?" she asked with a look of concern. "Are you okay? You look like skin and bones."

"I'm fine. You don't have to worry about me."

"It's that job, isn't it? You really need to slow down before that job kills you."

"No, Nana, it's not the job. Don't worry, okay?"

"Don't you tell me not to worry—you will always be my baby."

"I know, Nana. Where's Momma?"

"I don't know, child. You know your mother. She's probably out with some man or something. She still loves to run the streets..."

"Well, tell her I stopped by," he said, pulling out a wad of money from his front pocket. "Here, take this."

"Boy, put that money back in your pocket," she huffed. "We are fine."

"Nana, please, just take it. I know you all are struggling over here."

"I'm not taking your money, Mitchell. My social security takes care of me."

"What about Momma? I can't remember the last time she had a job."

"Your mother has always had a man to take care of her, so don't you even worry about her."

"Okay, I'll talk to you later, Nana..."

"Leaving so soon? Your sister is upstairs."

"Huh? Kia's here?"

"Yes, Son, and she'll be glad to see you."

"I doubt that very seriously. The last time I checked, she was still pissed at me for breaking up with Sandra."

"Boy, stop all that foolishness and go see about your sister. She's not doing so well and could really use somebody to talk to."

"Okay."

Mitch went upstairs to her sister's old room, and she was lying on the bed, crying. He sat on the bed and tried to comfort her. She hugged him and almost held him tight enough to stop his breathing.

"What's wrong, baby sis?" Mitch asked.

"It's nothing, Mitch," she answered, wiping off her face. "What brings you by?"

"I just came by to see Momma and Nana; that's all."

"Me, too, but Momma's running streets as usual."

"Yeah, some things never change. Look, I know we haven't been on the best of terms, but I just want to say that I'm sorry I hurt you, Kia. Sandra was your best friend, and I messed that up."

"You damn right you messed up, Mitch. What were you thinking? Sandra is a good woman, but you cheated on her with that tramp. Now, she doesn't even talk to me anymore."

"I know, and you're right. Brea and I broke up..."

"Left you high and dry, huh? Good. That gold-digging tramp hit the road as soon as you started having financial problems."

"Yeah, she dumped me. She got her record deal and dropped me like a bad habit."

"I can't say that I'm sorry about it because you're definitely better off without her. I gucss you now know how Sandra feels—you can't play with women's emotions like that."

"You know, I could really use a good lawyer to help me with my tax problems," Mitch said, quickly changing the subject. "Can you recommend one of your colleagues to me?"

"Say no more—I work with an attorney, who's the answer to your prayers. Her name is Susan McGovern, and she specializes in tax law. She'll deal with the IRS directly, and she'll be able to negotiate a reasonable payment plan with them for you and keep you out of jail."

"Thanks, sis. I really appreciate this."

"No problem, Mitch."

"Well, enough about me. Why were you crying?"

"I don't want to talk about it."

"Kia, don't be like that. You're always so private about your stuff and always in everybody else's business."

"No, I'm not, Mitch..."

"Then tell me what's going on with you."

"I broke up with my boyfriend today."

"I'm sorry to hear that. It seems to be the flavor of the month."

"You don't have to be sorry because it was for the best. He wasn't the person I thought he was."

"I know what you mean."

Kia paused and said, "Why can't men just tell the damn truth?"

"I don't know, sis. I used to be a habitual liar, and I would twist a story to suit my own purpose. Most people don't realize or care about hurting others until the same thing happens to them."

"My boyfriend came off as a nice guy, but the truth is that he was a killer and a drug dealer. He totally lied about who he was and what he did."

"How did you find out about it? Did you catch him doing something shady, or did he come clean about it?"

"He told me that he changed his whole life for me...that he had done some terrible things in his past and wanted to be a better person once he met me. I asked him what he meant by saying he had done terrible things, and he told me the truth."

"So, it basically never came up until today, right?"

"Right. And the funny thing is he had broken up with me first because he was tired of me flipping out on him because he can't handle a woman like me."

"Handle a woman like you? You're a man-eater, Kia. You get these men to fall for you, and then you break them down piece by piece. That gets old after a while."

"So, what you saying, Mitch? Am I supposed to just let a guy walk all over me?"

"Nah, that's not what I'm saying. You need to lighten up, or else nobody is gonna date you past six months."

There was brief silence, and then Kia said, "It was weird how we met, though. I met him the night Wes got killed at your club."

"Really?" Mitch asked as the creases in his forehead became more prominent. "How did you all meet?"

"It was the strangest thing," Kia answered. "He bought me a couple of drinks while I was sitting at the bar, and we hit it off instantly. We danced for a little while, and he made me laugh the entire time we were together. Once he had gone to the bathroom, I never saw him again that night."

"Did he go the men's room right before the robbery?"

"Yes, as a matter of fact, he did."

"Do you remember anything about the robbery?"

"I didn't see a thing. I got out of there as soon as I heard the first gunshot."

Kia took a deep breath and said, "Do you think he had something to do with the robbery and murder of our cousin?"

"I don't know, but I'm gonna get to the bottom of what happened that night. Where does this dude stay? Somebody is gonna pay for what happened to Wes if it's the last thing I do."

"No, Mitch, I can't tell you that. We don't know what Norris is capable of. What if something happens to you?"

"His name is Norris?"

"Yes, his name is Norris Adams. Why?"

"Well, since you won't tell me where he lives, I can give his name to the police."

"Are you going to the police station right now? If you are, I want to go with you."

"No, not right now because I was just there earlier today, but I'm gonna give the police his name once I leave here."

"Okay, give me a call at work or call my cell once you know something."

"You'll be the first to know, sis. I hope your man didn't have anything to do with this."

"We're done, Mitch, so if he's responsible for Wesley's death in any way, let the chips fall where they may."

"That's all I needed to hear. See you later."

"Bye, Mitch."

He kissed her on the cheek and hurried down the stairs. Nana was in the kitchen cooking some food and stopped what she was doing once she heard Mitch coming from upstairs.

"See you later, Nana," Mitch said.

"Are you going to stay for dinner?" Nana asked.

"I'm sorry, Nana. I can't. Tell Momma I said hello."

"Alright, Mitchell. Don't be a stranger, okay?"

"I won't."

Mitch left the house and scurried to his car. His plan was to call the police, so they could run Norris's name through their database, but the police called him before he could put the car in drive.

"Hello?" Mitch asked.

"Hey, Mitch, it's Detective Grimes again. I have some bad news for you."

"What is it?"

"We released Bria Jones a couple of hours ago."

"Huh? Why?"

"She passed the polygraph test, and we don't have any other evidence that links her to the crime."

"Dammit! She was the one who planted those guns in my club because her own sister admitted it to me."

"I'm sorry, Mitch, but it's basically your word against hers, and unfortunately, that's not enough to hold her in custody at this present time. I can promise you that we will continue to search for other leads in this case, and I'll be in touch."

"Okay, Detective Grimes, thank you."

Mitch disconnected the call and pounded his fist on the dashboard. He called Cedric after giving himself a minute or so to regroup.

"Hey, Ced," Mitch said.

"Mitch," Cedric said. "Talk to me."

"I think I know who another one of the crew members is."

"Yeah? Who is it?"

"His name is Norris Adams, and he used to mess around with my sister."

"You think he's part of the clique, huh?"

"I don't know for sure, but he was at the club with my sister the night it got robbed. He disappeared right before it happened."

"Really? Where does this punk live?"

"I don't know. Kia wouldn't tell me because she's worried about my safety."

"Okay, don't worry about it. I'll see what I can find out about this dude and get back to you."

"Alright, Ced. Peace."

Mitch quickly drove off after ending the call—destination unknown. His heart started racing, his head started pounding, and he began to sweat profusely. Bria's release from police custody was the last straw—the overload of emotions and stress caused him to blackout temporarily. However, he never lost consciousness and found himself driving northbound on the Bishop Ford Expressway shortly afterwards, not remembering how he got there.

Part of him wanted to hunt down Bria and put a bullet in her head for the part she played in Wesley's death, but the other part of him—the core values that Nana had instilled in him ultimately prevailed. The charming, fun-loving Mitch was definitely gone, and a cold, sullen Mitch had emerged from the ashes of a broken heart.

43

The Kappas had decided to take advantage of the unseasonably eighty-degree weather by throwing a yard party in front of Washington Hall, and one of the Southern University campus DJ's was spinning on the turntables. It was dinnertime, and students were hanging out and listening to the music. The atmosphere was lively, the girls were looking fresh, and the Kappas were doing their thing, stepping and twirling their red and white canes.

Max slowly searched the crowd to see if he could spot Spider but had no luck. However, he recognized a few of the students who frequented his barbershop weekly, and one of the guys walked up to him and gave him some dap.

"What's up, Max?" the guy asked.

"It's all good, Kevin," Max replied. "Y'all got the yard bumpin' today."

"Yeah, just a little something the Kappas are throwing."

"Have you seen Spider?"

"Nah, I haven't seen him today. He might be around here somewhere, though."

"Aiight, catch you later."

"Peace."

Max continued to walk around, hoping to run into Spider, so he could settle the score for robbing Jill. His intent was to scare him, not kill him, for fear of unwanted attention from local authorities. *The Three Musketeers*—Piru, Spider, and Bam were nowhere to be found, so he headed over to Jones Hall to see if they might be shooting ball. The whole college scene didn't appeal to him anymore, and he felt somewhat out of place because of the fact that he was knocking on thirty's door, even though he barely looked over twenty-one.

There were some guys playing when Max arrived at the basketball courts, and as luck would have it, Spider was there without his two sidekicks. Max casually walked in the middle of the court and interrupted their game. He laughed out loud once one of the guys began cursing him out.

"Man, what the hell you doing?" the guy asked. "Get off the court before I beat the brakes off you!"

"Look here, college boy, I don't have no beef with you," Max said calmly, "so back the hell up before I make an example outta you."

"Dude, get off the court, so we can finish our game," another guy said.

"Why am I here, Spider?" Max asked.

"How the hell should I know, Max?" he asked. "Why *are* you here?"

"You should never...ever...answer a question with a question," Max answered angrily. "Lemme paint a picture for you. My wife got robbed at that beauty shop on Plank Road, and I know for a fact you did it."

"So, what if I did, man?" Spider asked, inching his way toward Max and stretching his long arms up in the air and away from his torso. "What are you gonna do about it?"

"You don't have any idea who I am, do you?" Max asked.

Spider pulled out his switchblade and said, "I'mma take your money, too, punk."

Max raised up his Clyde Drexler Rockets jersey to reveal his .380 semi-automatic tucked inside his blue jean shorts. Spider retracted his knife in surrender and began to back away.

"Never bring a knife to a gunfight, homeboy," Max said. "I'mma give you a pass because you didn't know who you were sticking up today. Give me my money back, and I'll forget about the whole thing."

"My bad, Max, I didn't know," Spider said, pulling the two hundred dollars cash that he had out of his pocket and handing it to Max. "You got it."

"You gentleman have a nice day," Max said as he put the money in his pocket and walked away.

The six wannabe ballplayers were speechless until Curtis, the first guy who threatened to dismember Max, said, "What did you do, Spider? I thought you stopped taking penitentiary chances like that out here."

"Don't worry about what I be doing," Spider said. "Let's just finish the game."

"Man, forget this game," one of the other guys said. "You almost got your head blown off, and you're talking about finishing the game. I left Little Rock, Arkansas to avoid this ghetto madness, man—I'm out."

"Me, too," Curtis added. "Later fellas."

"The hell with y'all, then," Spider said as the rest of the guys cleared the court and walked in the direction of the yard party.

Spider looked on as they disappeared in the crowd of students a football field away. He decided to join the campus festivities after weighing his options. His anger and embarrassment of being punked didn't deter him from wanting to hang out and look at the eye candy dressed in tube tops, painted-on jeans, daisy dukes, and mini-skirts.

He strolled toward Washington Hall and spotted his crew standing by the one of the speakers on the left side of the dorm entrance. He could see Piru's gold teeth glistening in the sunlight.

"Where you been?" Piru asked. "It's chicks for days out here."

"I was hooping in back of Jones Hall with some of the fellas," Spider answered. "What's up, Bam?"

"It's all good," Bam answered. "What's the deal, homie? You look like you're ready to kill somebody."

"I am," Spider said. "That dude from the barbershop named Max pulled a gun on me and took my money. We need to step up our game and get some hardware."

"What?" Piru asked. "Max pulled a gun on you?"

"Yeah, I didn't know I robbed his wife by that beauty shop on Plank Road," Spider replied. "He stepped on the court talking out the side of his neck, so I pulled my knife out on him, and that's when he showed his gun."

"Damn, man, you robbed his wife?" Bam asked. "You're lucky he didn't shoot you, man. Hell, I would've unloaded my clip on you if that was me."

"Man, shut up," Spider said. "Whose side are you on, anyway?"

"Chill, y'all," Piru urged. "I'll handle this—mark my words, Spider, but we have more important business to discuss."

"What business?" Spider asked.

"Not here, man," Piru said, "but you're right. It's time to elevate our game, and that's exactly what we're gonna do."

44

"Now boarding flight 398 to New York," the ticket agent said. "Please have your boarding pass ready."

Brea hopped up from her seat and walked toward the line that formed by the gate. She handed the agent her boarding pass and ticket once she got to the front of the line and entered the plane. The plane was half-full, and she had a window seat in the middle of the plane to her left. She placed her carry-on bag in the overhead cabin and took her seat.

It was then that she noticed a very attractive man walking down the aisle—he was tall, he had a muscular physique, and he had a distinct jaw line. His golden-brown complexion and jet-black wavy hair turned Brea on—he looked like someone straight out of a GQ magazine. Please sit next to me, she thought, because it was lust at first sight for her.

He placed his bag in the overhead bin right above her head, and she could smell the masculine scent of his cologne. She never took her eyes off him the entire time he was trying to get situated. It was as if she was burning a hole on the side of his face with her eyes, and he turned to face her once he sat one seat away from her in the same row. He smiled, and she smiled back at him before he reached in his bag and pulled out some Beats by Dre earphones.

"I'm Brea Jones," she said abruptly.

"Josh Rivera," he said, extending his hand to her. "Nice to meet you."

"Nice to meet you, too," she said, biting her bottom lip suggestively. "I hope I'm not coming on too strong, but I'd like to get to know you better."

"You're very beautiful, Brea, and no, I don't think you're coming on too strong. You seem like a woman who knows how to get what she wants."

"I am indeed, and I think you're very handsome, Josh."

"Thank you."

"What do you do?"

"Well, I'm an underwear model. I've done photo shoots for Fruit of the Loom, and now I'm with Calvin Klein."

"Wow, that's very impressive. I can totally see you modeling underwear."

"What do you do?" he asked, laughing.

"I'm sorry, what I meant to say was..."

"It's okay...I'm not embarrassed because I really like what I do."

"That's great, Josh. I'm a singer, and I'm shooting my first music video tomorrow morning."

"Damn, that's dope, Brea. I'll definitely be looking out for your video."

"Are you from New York?"

"Not originally. My family is originally from Puerto Rico, and I grew up in Chicago. I moved to New York to pursue my dream a couple of years ago—I came back to town to celebrate my brother's birthday."

"Have you always wanted to be a model?"

"No, I want to be an actor someday. Modeling is just a stepping stone to greener pastures."

"Please fasten your seatbelts," one of the flight attendants said.

The other flight attendant began giving the safety tutorial, and Brea said, "Why don't you sit next to me? It looks like no one is going to be sitting here."

"Okay," he replied, his grin transforming into a smile.

Josh's radiant smile captivated Brea, and she had never believed in love at first sight until that very moment. They talked the whole flight, and it seemed as if they had known each other for years. She had a connection with him that she never felt with anyone else—not even with Mitch. They accompanied each other to baggage claim in the JFK Airport and walked outside to catch an Uber once they got their luggage.

"What are you doing later?" Josh asked. "Maybe we can go out for drinks or something."

"I don't have anything planned," Brea answered, "and yes, I'd love to have some drinks with you."

"Great, I know a place in Brooklyn that serves the best Long Island Ice Teas in town."

"Okay, lead the way. And just so you know, I grew up in Brooklyn."

Josh requested the Uber driver on his app, and they went to his place in Brooklyn to drop off their luggage, and then they headed to the bar. There was a live band playing there, and they downed shot after shot until a little after midnight. They had begun making out as the overflow of alcohol had them feeling free and uninhibited. Not wasting another minute, they had decided to take the party back to Josh's apartment.

Their steamy passion ignited while they were in the living room kissing and groping each other, and needless to say, they never made it to the bedroom. They stripped each other down to the bare essentials, and their lovemaking session continued until they were completely drained. They lay naked drenched in sweat on the living room floor momentarily until Josh got up and went to the bathroom to retrieve a couple of towels, so they could wipe themselves off.

She sat on the floor in awe of his muscular body as he walked toward her and handed her a towel. She felt as though she had won the lottery and hoped he felt the same way.

"Here, you can use this to dry off," he said.

"Thank you," she said.

"Where have you been all of my life?" he asked and smiled.

"I was just thinking the exact same thing," she replied. "Now that I'm back in New York, we'll have to figure out what this thing is between us."

"I don't know what this thing is, but I do know that I like it. Are you seeing anyone?"

"No, I just broke up with my boyfriend before I left Chicago. And you?"

"I'm not with anyone because my schedule hasn't allowed me to meet anybody special...at least not until I met you."

"Aw, that is so sweet, Josh. I'd love to keep seeing you...to see where this relationship takes us."

“Are we in a relationship?” he said, smile turning into a wide grin.

“I sincerely hope so,” she said, smiling coyly back at him. “Do you believe in love at first sight?”

“Before today, no, but now I definitely do.”

45

Mitch was lying on his bed, flicking channels. Nothing sparked his interest, so he grabbed a beer out of the mini-refrigerator sitting on top of the dresser. He twisted off the cap and tossed it in the plastic garbage can next to the bed. He took a swig and rolled his head back on the bedpost. Still no word from Cedric. Damn. It had been over three weeks, and Mitch hadn't heard a word from him. Mitch tried Cedric's cell phone and stopped by a few of his businesses, but nobody had heard from him or knew his whereabouts.

He got up from the bed and walked toward the window of his diminutive room at an extended-stay hotel on the north side of Chicago. He looked to his right and saw the light turn green a half-block down, and a woman pushing a baby stroller crossed the street. It was a few minutes after nine o'clock at night, and the streets were tranquil in the midst of the darkness and freezing cold wind on a Sunday night.

He quickly grew tired of staring out the window and walked toward the bathroom, where his suitcase occupied space in a corner on the floor. He reached inside it and pulled out the nine-millimeter pistol that he inherited from his cousin, Wesley. He tucked it in his pants and put on his leather jacket. He then exited his room and went downstairs to the lobby and out the door. His car was parked across the street—he usually had to hike a couple of blocks because parking on the north side of town was scarce.

"If you wanna do something right, you have to do it yourself," he said to himself.

He had found a business address for Norris a few days earlier and decided to case the place before making his move on him. Norris had posted flyers of his business in some of the restaurants and grocery stores on the south side, and Mitch luckily found one of his flyers inside an Italian beef spot that he had frequented in the past. Someone was going to pay for the robbery and murder of his cousin and six bouncers, and he was going to start with Norris. He assumed it was a residence because the address was on the seventy-eighth hundred block of Aberdeen in the Auburn Gresham neighborhood.

He continued to let his car warm up for another five minutes before heading east toward Lakeshore Drive. He devised the plan of calling Norris to talk about his relationship with his sister Kia in order for Norris to let his guard down somewhat. Mitch planned on pretending that Kia was heartbroken over their breakup and wanted to work things out with Norris, and then he was going to gut-punch him by implicating him in the robbery of his club and Wesley's murder.

He pulled his phone out of his pocket and dialed Norris's number while at a stoplight.

"Hello?" Norris asked. "Who's this?"

"Hey, Norris, this is Mitch," he said, "Kia's brother. Can we talk?"

"Talk about what, man? Me and your sister are over."

"I know," Mitch paused, "but she's really heartbroken over your breakup. I was hoping I could talk you into reconsidering—come on. I'll buy you a drink at the *50 Yard Line*."

"I have a busy day tomorrow," Norris said. "Thanks, but no thanks, bruh."

"Look, you seem like a cool brother, Norris, and I never got a chance to meet you. My sister is really sorry, and she loves you to death. Just have a drink with me, all right?"

"Okay, man, I'll meet you there in about a half-hour."

"Alright, see you there."

Mitch disconnected the call and said to himself, "That was easy. This dude isn't gonna know what hit him."

46

She kissed him passionately on his lips and neck while they snuggled on the living room sofa. They had been watching a DVD of the movie *Girls Trip* and had a full bowl of popcorn and two half-empty sodas on the living room table. They were more into each other than the movie, and they consciously had to refrain from tearing off each other's clothes, so they could enjoy watching the remainder of it.

Brea went to the kitchen to get them two more sodas out of the fridge, and that's when she noticed a line of what appeared to be cocaine on the kitchen counter. She tried to dismiss it, but her instincts wouldn't let her disregard what she saw.

"Baby, what's this on the kitchen counter?" Brea asked.

"What did you say?" Josh asked, walking toward the kitchen. "Oh, yeah, I was frying some chicken earlier, and I forgot to wipe up the flour by the kitchen sink."

Josh quickly got a damp paper towel and wiped off the counter, and Brea looked in the fridge again and noticed the plastic bowl full of fried chicken. She belted out a sigh of relief and said, "I love you, Josh."

"I love you, too," Josh said. "I'm so happy you moved in with me. I never want to let you go."

"I'm not going anywhere, sweetheart. I start my tour soon, and I hope you can take some time off to be with me."

"I'm definitely going to try, baby. I won't be able to accompany you for the entire tour, but I'll be there for a good deal of it."

"Wonderful, I'll take whatever I can get."

"How was your studio session today?"

"Long and hard, but I was able to lay all my tracks down."

"That's great, babe."

Josh paused and said, "By the way, what's up with your crazy ex stalking you? I think I saw him one day outside the apartment while I was on my way to a photo shoot."

"He's not my ex. I fired him as my manager, and he didn't take it too well."

"I'm just saying, baby, the dude won't go away quietly..."

"Don't worry about him. He's nobody. I told him what was up, so I hope he gets the message."

"Well, he better stay away from you, or I'm going have to say something to him."

"Please don't go anywhere near him, okay?"

"Only if he stays away from you, Brea."

He pulled her closer and kissed her passionately. He stopped himself momentarily and reached in his pocket.

"Why did you stop?" she asked. "I want you so bad."

He opened the case that he retrieved from his pocket and showed her a ring. Her mouth gaped open as he fell to one knee.

"You are the one, Brea," he said. "I want to spend the rest of my life with you, and I don't want to waste any more time."

"Yes, baby, yes! I will marry you!"

He placed the five-carat ring on her finger, and it fit perfectly. He then rose from the floor and took her hand.

"This ring is absolutely beautiful, Josh. You have great taste."

"Thank you. I'm glad you like it because you're worth it."

"Make love to me, baby," she said.

He picked her up and whisked her away to the bedroom. He wasted no time ripping off her tube top bra and tight-fitting sweat pants, and they began exploring every inch of each other's bodies. They made love until they climaxed multiple times, and he temporarily lost the power of speech.

"You like that, daddy?" she asked confidently.

He took a deep breath and replied, "You already know the answer to that."

"I thought so," she smiled.

"Let's go out and celebrate our engagement tonight. I feel on top of the world right now."

"Not tonight, baby, because I got an early day tomorrow—a photo shoot with XXL, and Hot 97 wants to interview me for the upcoming album."

"No problem, I understand. Maybe tomorrow night then, okay?"

"That's sounds great. We can invite some of our friends and make it a party...maybe I could have my sister fly in from Chicago."

He kissed her on the cheek and said, "The more, the merrier. I'll call my two brothers and my sister tonight to see if they can fly in tomorrow."

They continued to lie in bed and savor the moment of blissfulness. He stroked her hair while she caressed his stomach. The scent of her perfume and hair had captivated him from the moment they met, and the ripples of his abdomen mesmerized her since the first time they made love. They had fallen asleep in each another's arms before they realized it a half-hour later.

47

"How many books you got?" Max asked. "Because I ain't got nothing."

"I ain't got nothing, either," Tyrone answered. "I guess it's board then."

"Damn, I thought y'all could play," Jimmy said. "Me and my girl are about to run a Boston on y'all."

"I don't have anything either, baby," Tisha added.

"Don't worry. I got this," Jimmy said.

"We'll see," Tyrone said.

Max and Tyrone were losing badly to Jimmy and Tisha in a game of spades while Tyrone's girlfriend, Melissa, and Jill were in the kitchen frying chicken and French fries for everybody. The six of them had made a ritual of getting together every other day since Jill and Tisha met at the beauty salon three weeks ago. The clique hung out at Club Infiniti last night, and they went to the dollar show the night before last to see *John Wick 2*.

Jill and Tisha were the glue to the whole clique, but subsets within the group were forming as well. Some were perfectly innocent, but one in particular wasn't so innocent. Max and Tyrone were still as tight as ever, Jill and Melissa had grown closer due to the fact that both of them loved cooking, and Max and Jimmy had an affinity for basketball. However, Tisha had her eyes on Max, and she would do subtle things when he was around, like drop something on purpose and bend over right in front of him. He would always try to play it off by looking in the other direction or pretending like he didn't see her. She would also smile and wink at him whenever the opportunity presented itself.

"I'm out," Max said. "I can't believe I got a crappy hand every damn deal."

"Don't blame it on the hand," Jimmy added. "I got skills, money."

"Whatever," Tyrone said. "We can take this to the asphalt and settle this once and for all."

"I'm going in the kitchen to check on the girls," Tisha said and walked away.

"You definitely don't wanna go there, Jimmy," Max said. "Nobody could check me in the entire SWAC Conference when I played."

"That was then, Max," Jimmy said. "It's my time now."

"I'm not washed up yet," Max said, getting some dap from Tyrone. "We're gonna play for some money when the season is over."

"It's a bet," Jimmy said.

"What seed you think y'all gonna get in the NCAA tournament?" Tyrone asked.

"Once we win the SWAC Tournament, we'll probably get a sixteenth seed," Jay said.

"Confident, aren't we?" Max asked rhetorically. "Y'all probably gonna get Kansas or Villanova if y'all make it."

"I ain't worried, bro," Jimmy said. "We get whoever we get, and I'mma bring my A-game regardless."

"No doubt," Max said. "Hey, are we outta beer?"

"I'm afraid so," Tyrone said.

Max walked into the kitchen and checked the refrigerator—only one beer left.

"I'll be back, baby," Max said. "I'm gonna make a beer run."

"Hurry back because the food will be ready soon," Jill urged.

"I won't be long," Max said.

"Lemme ride with you," Tisha said. "I need to get some things for the shop, and you'll save me the trip."

"Uh, okay," Max said, looking at Jill for her reaction.

"Bring me back some nail polish remover if you can, Tisha," Jill said.

"I got you," Tisha said as she walked out of the kitchen. "I'mma ride with Max to the store to get some stuff for the shop, baby."

"That's cool, babe," Jimmy said. "Bring me back some gummy bears."

"Okay, baby," Tisha said.

Max and Tisha left the house, and they took Jill's truck because Max's truck was blocked in the driveway. He unlocked the doors with the alarm button and opened his door to get in.

"Aren't you gonna open my car door for me?" Tisha said, trying to give Max her most captivating smile.

And captivating she was—five-foot-eight, a slim but shapely body, and the most beautiful and alluring smile that Max had ever seen. Her short and sassy blonde hair reflected her personality, and her caramel skin was soft and smooth. Max tried to fight his unbridled attraction to her, but it was virtually useless.

"I'm sorry, Tisha, that wasn't very gentlemanly of me," he answered.

"No, it wasn't, but I won't hold it against you," she said.

He walked over to her side to open the door, and she backed up ever so slightly and brushed her wide hips and plump derriere against his groin. She held it there momentarily while rummaging through her purse for some lip gloss, and he felt his nature rise instantly and fought like hell to contain himself. She then sat down in the truck and smiled at him as he shut her door for her. He trotted to the driver side door and abruptly sat down in the driver's seat, and she giggled to herself. It was her whole intent—she brushed up against him to get a reaction, and she wasn't disappointed.

The scent of her perfume permeated the truck even with the windows down, and the smell of it intoxicated him. How could this be happening? His thoughts raced in his head—he imagined what her breasts looked like behind her tight-fitting blue t-shirt that had the word DIVA inscribed on it, and her jeans were so tight that they looked like they were practically painted on.

"Max!" she shouted to get his attention.

"Huh?" he asked, snapping out of his fantasy.

"I called your named three times. Are you all right?"

"Sorry about that. I was trying to figure out what liquor store got Budweiser on sale."

"Oh, okay. Why are you worried about a sale? Aren't you and Jill ballin'?"

"I'm trying to hold on to what we got, not blow all of it."

"Don't tell me you're one of those cheap brothers, are you?"

"Nah, ma, not at all. I give Jill whatever she wants."

"That's good to know."

"Where you wanna go? There's a beauty supply store not far from here."

"That's cool. We can go there."

Max put Jill's black 2018 Infiniti QX80 in drive and slowly drove off. It was still relatively warm, even though the sun had set, but there was an ever so slight breeze that made the humidity bearable.

"So, you and Jill have been together since college, huh?"

"Yeah, almost ten years. We just got married last year."

"That's great, Max. You two look great together."

"Thanks. What about you and Jimmy?"

"We've been together two years, and our daughter will be one in June. We're gonna get married once we graduate."

"That's great...y'all seem to have a good relationship."

She put her hand on Max's thigh and asked, "What about your relationship?"

"What about it?" he asked.

"Do you love Jill or are you *in love* with her?"

He removed her hand from his thigh and said, "I thought y'all were friends, Tisha."

"We are friends, but what our significant others don't know won't hurt them."

"Look, I don't know what's going on between us, but I can't go there with you. I love Jill, and I don't wanna mess up what we have."

She started caressing his thigh this time and said, "Are you trying to convince me, or are you trying to convince yourself?"

"What are you trying to say?"

"Come on—I'm not blind. I see the way you look at me."

He pulled over into a convenience store parking lot and took her hand. He leaned in and planted a kiss on her, and she opened her mouth completely for the French kiss that she so desperately wanted. Their kindred, degenerate spirits were drawn to each other like a magnet to metal as they kissed for what seemed like an eternity. The line had been crossed, and there was no going back.

He continued to kiss her lips, cheeks, and neck before he abruptly pulled himself away from her. She looked confused and tried to pull him close, but he refused her. He then tried to catch his breath and wrap his mind around what had just happened. She pulled down the passenger side sun visor to check her makeup.

"Why did you stop?" she asked.

"I can't do this," he answered.

"Yes, you can," she said. "We're gonna finish this tomorrow night. This was just a sample, baby."

"I don't think that's a good idea, Tisha," he said. "What just happened can never happen again."

"What do you mean this can never happen again? I really like you, Max, and I know you feel the same way about me."

"You know that I want you in the worst way, babe, but what if they find out?"

"They won't...this can just be our thing. We can get together once a week, and you can pick the place."

"Okay, you win. We can hook up tomorrow."

He paused momentarily and said, "Let's hurry up and get your stuff from the beauty supply store before everybody starts getting suspicious."

They stopped at the beauty supply store to get her merchandise, and the liquor store was across the street. They got back to the house and realized that an hour had passed, and all eyes were on them once they entered the front door.

"What took y'all so long?" Tyrone asked.

"Yeah, baby, the food is cold," Jill added.

"I couldn't find what I was looking for at first," Tisha interjected, "so we had to go to another store."

Max tried to hide his guilt and said, "Who wants to play some Dominos?"

"I'm game," Jimmy said.

"Me, too," Tyrone said.

"I got class tomorrow, sweetheart," Melissa said to Tyrone. "We really need to get going."

"Okay, baby," Tyrone said. "Sorry, y'all, we gotta bounce."

"Here are your gummy bears, baby," Tisha said. "We're gonna go, too. I got an eight o'clock calculus class."

Jill gave Tisha a hug and said, "I'll talk to you tomorrow."

They said their goodbyes, and Max went outside to see everybody off while Jill checked on the baby. Max lit a cigarette and stayed outside for a few minutes longer. He was overwhelmed with guilt because he broke his promise to Jill that he'd never cheat on her again. He knew, if she ever found out about what he did with Tisha, their relationship would definitely be in jeopardy.

48

Mitch stepped inside the bar and searched for Norris. He checked his watch, and it read four minutes before midnight. He had remembered Kia describing the way Norris looked when she first started dating him, but nobody fit the bill at first glance.

A live band was playing jazz, and Mitch had decided to grab a seat at the bar facing the door, so he could examine every patron who entered and exited the club. It was relatively crowded for a Sunday night, and he felt slightly out of place because he was dressed casually while most of the people were in their Sunday best.

"What you drinking?" the bartender asked.

"Let me get a Bud Light," Mitch answered.

Mitch continued to watch the people come in and out the front entrance, and a guy matching Kia's description walked in. Mitch grabbed his beer and napkin that the bartender had placed on the counter and walked toward the guy. He was about the same height as Mitch, he was light-skinned, and he sported a tapered mini-afro. It appeared that Kia had picked a guy who resembled her brother. The dead giveaway was a three-inch scar on his right jaw that she said he had—it was the one and only thing that she didn't like about his appearance.

"Norris?" Mitch asked, extending his hand.

"Yeah," he answered, shaking Mitch's hand. "You're Kia's brother, Mitch, huh?"

"In the flesh. What you drinking?"

"I'll have what you're drinking."

"Cool, I'll be right back."

Mitch went back to the bar and ordered another Bud Light and two shots of Crown Royal. Norris had picked a table closest to the entrance—a subtle hint that he didn't plan on staying long.

"I bought you a shot of whiskey, too," Mitch said.

"That's cool," Norris said, downing the shot immediately before twisting the cap off his beer. "So, what do you wanna talk about, homeboy?"

"You, my friend, tell me a little about yourself."

"What you wanna know?"

"For starters, what do you do for a living?"

"I'm a carpenter, and I rehab houses for a living."

"Man, that's the lick. You make a lot of dough, huh?"

"I do okay."

"So, what's up with you and Kia?"

"Like I said over the phone, we're over."

"No chance of you all working things out?"

"I'm afraid not, Mitch."

"But Kia told me that she wants you back."

"What? If Kia wants me back so bad, why hasn't she returned any of my calls?"

"You tried to call her?"

"Yeah, several times, but she doesn't seem that heartbroken to me. I'm confused, bruh."

"Maybe you should try to reach out to her again..."

"It takes two, my man."

"I used to own a club similar to this one once upon a time," Mitch said, changing the subject.

"Yeah?" Norris asked. "What happened to it?"

"You know, I ask myself that question every day. One minute, everything is fine, and then the next thing I know, the Feds raid my club."

"Really?"

"Yeah, and that's only the half of it—the IRS seized everything I own."

"Damn, man, that's jacked up."

"You're damn right it's jacked up. I don't have a pot to piss in literally. I'm staying in a hotel."

"Look, man, I'm sympathetic to your situation, and I'm truly sorry about what happened to you. However, I don't really have time for this conversation, so I'm gonna bounce. Nice meeting you, Mitch."

"You don't have time? But you had time to rob my damn club last year, didn't you, Norris?"

"What did you say?"

Mitch pulled out his Glock and pointed it directly at Norris's forehead, and this caused much of the crowd to panic and flee the bar. Norris quickly held his hands up in surrender.

"I didn't stutter, Norris. I know for a fact that you and your crew robbed my club and killed seven people that night."

"Man, I don't know what the hell you're talking about—who told you that?"

"Okay, here's how it's gonna go down—either you're gonna tell me where Max is, or I'm gonna splatter your damn brains all over the wall behind you. You decide."

"I said I don't know what you're talking about, man!"

"The police are gonna be here any minute, so you have five seconds to answer my damn question!" Mitch shouted, racking the slide of his nine-millimeter pistol.

"Okay, I'll tell you! Max—he's in Baton Rouge, Louisiana. He owns a barbershop near the Southern University campus..."

"You see, that wasn't so hard, was it? And for the record, Kia doesn't want anything to do with you, bruh. As a matter of fact, stay as far away from her as humanly possible, or I'll kill you."

Mitch lowered his gun and fled the club, and he hopped inside his car and sped off. He heard sirens, and he could see the flashing blue and red lights about a half-mile east of the club. He hit the Dan Ryan expressway, which was west of the club, in less than a minute and was ghost.

49

There was a packed house at the barbershop late Monday morning. Max was backed up, Tyrone had a full plate, and the other three barbers in the shop had a boatload of appointments for the day. Business was booming, and Max had thoughts of expanding the operation. Perhaps a move to a strip mall location was in the future, but not too far from campus because the students were their bread and butter.

Tisha was still on Max's mind, but he didn't have time to focus on her. They were supposed to link up in the early evening, but he was having second thoughts. His crazy attraction to her was overriding his common sense because he told Jill a lie about a bogus business meeting with a potential partner who wanted to invest in his shop.

"I'mma hit that this week guaranteed," one of the patrons said. "I've been putting in work all month, and it's gonna pay off."

"You ain't gonna hit nothing, Clyde," Tyrone said as he lined the back of his head. "If she really liked you, you wouldn't have to work this hard."

"Shut up, Big Ty," Clyde said. "You lucked up on your girl anyway. She is way too fine for you."

"You're just a hater, man," Tyrone said. "I bet you ten bucks that you don't hit that girl, and besides, I saw her kicking it with that Alpha dude last week."

"Whatever, man," Clyde said. "It's a race to the finish line, so may the best man win."

"You aiight over there, Max?" Tyrone asked.

"Yeah, I'm cool," Max answered.

"What really took y'all so long last night?" Tyrone asked.

"What you talking about?" Max asked.

"Come on, man," Tyrone stated. "I see the way Tisha be looking at you and everything. You hit that, didn't you?"

"Hell nah, man," Max answered. "It ain't that deep. Jimmy is my man, and I wouldn't do that to him."

"Oh, okay," Tyrone said. "Just making sure you ain't holding out on me."

Tyrone finished Clyde's hair, Clyde tipped him and gave him dap, and it was on to the next customer. Max was still working on his customer, and the shop was now filled to capacity. Then out of the blue, Piru, Bam and Spider walked in.

"Appointments only today," Tyrone said. "We're booked for the rest of the day."

"We're not here for a haircut," Piru said.

"Then why are you here?" Max asked tersely. "I'm done playing games with you, Piru."

"This ain't no game, homie," Spider said. "We got some unfinished business."

Max pulled out his pistol and aimed it at Piru's head. The people in the shop scattered like roaches in daylight; Bam, Spider, and Tyrone all drew their guns.

"So, this is how it's gonna be, playa?" Piru asked.

"That's how you made it," Tyrone answered. "State your business or be gone, dude."

"Stand down, y'all," Piru said.

Bam and Spider lowered their guns, and Max and Tyrone followed suit.

"What do y'all want?" Max asked. "You just killed all my business."

"You embarrassed my man Spider, and that wasn't cool, Max," Piru answered. "I thought we had an understanding..."

"Spider played himself when he robbed my wife," Max stated. "You really don't have a clue about who you're dealing with. I bury bustas like you for breakfast, lunch and dinner."

"And I bury bustas like you, too," Piru said. "I'm Compton's finest..."

"Man, who you fooling?" Tyrone asked rhetorically. "Stop lying—we all know you grew up in Baldwin Hills, and both of your parents are lawyers. You need to quit trying to portray this fake gangsta image, bruh."

"I'll show you who's gangsta," Piru said.

"Hey, hey," Max urged. "What do you want, Piru? An apology? If anything, your man owes me an apology."

"That's not gonna happen," Spider said.

"All right, let's cut to the chase then," Bam said. "We're charging every business around here rent, so you owe us ten percent, Max. This is now our territory, and you clowns are gonna respect it."

"Y'all must be joking," Max said.

"This ain't no joke," Piru said. "It's our way or the highway, homeboy."

"Get outta my shop!" Max shouted.

"Okay, we're leaving, but we will be back," Piru said. "I can promise you that."

They left the shop, and Max and Tyrone were all that remained. Max looked at Tyrone and asked, "Can you believe this, Mack?"

"Yeah, these college boys are gonna try *us*."

"Are you thinking what I'm thinking?"

"I'm way ahead of you. It's time to take out the trash."

50

Brea was at a beauty shop in Harlem treating herself to a manicure and pedicure. She had plans with Josh, friends, and family later that night—dancing and celebrating at one of the hottest nightclubs at an undisclosed location in Brooklyn to celebrate their engagement. Bria had just flown in from Chicago to celebrate with them, and Josh's brother Steve was flying in later that afternoon.

She paid the technician and left the shop, and she was headed to a boutique not far away to shop for an outfit and home afterwards to get ready. Josh had some errands to run, so everyone was going to meet at the club later. She went to the corner to flag down a cab, and Brent appeared out of nowhere.

"What are you doing here, Brent?" Brea asked. "I thought I made myself clear."

"You used me, dammit!" Brent shouted.

"It's business, nothing personal," Brea said. "I'm just doing what the record label suggested, and that was to get a more experienced manager."

"You wouldn't even have a record deal if it wasn't for me, and now you just wanna cut me out of the deal."

"I'm sorry if you see things that way because I really appreciate everything you've done for me."

"I don't wanna hear that BS, Brea. You owe me!"

"What do you want, Brent?"

"I want us—I want things to be the way they used to be, baby. I love you."

"I can't do this with you—please—just give me some space."

"I know you have somebody else, but that's okay. Things can still be the same..."

"No, they can't, Brent. Look, I know we didn't sign any type of contract, but I promise I won't leave you out in the cold."

"It's not about the money, Brea. I've invested a lot of time in you, and I thought you were in it for the long haul."

"I did, too, but things change. You got way too close when I warned you not to do that. It's not my fault you fell in love with me, and I'm truly sorry that I broke your heart because it wasn't my intention."

"My heart's not broken, and I'm a big boy, Brea. I needed to know if there was any chance for us...I just needed some closure."

"No hard feelings, okay?"

"Sure, Brea, no feelings."

They embraced, and Brock kissed her on the forehead before crossing the street and heading in the direction of the subway.

"Take care of yourself," he said. "I wish you nothing but success."

"Thank you, Brent. Goodbye."

Brent disappeared into the crowd of people walking down the subway stairs as Brea looked on. She was relieved that she had finally gotten through to him, but she was also sad because she really did care about him. She also found herself thinking a lot about Mitch—she had a bad habit of ending relationships abruptly without dealing with the residual feelings she still had for the men who used to be in her life. She felt guilty about leaving Mitch at his lowest point, and she still loved him, even though she was now in love with Josh.

She was finally able to catch a cab after standing on the corner for about five minutes. She was starting to wrap her mind around actually getting married—the excitement of Josh's proposal had worn off, and reality had set in. She was also feeling mixed emotions—she might have possibly jumped the gun by saying yes because there was still a great deal that she didn't know about him, but she also knew it might be jitters because of the fact that no guy ever proposed to her.

Gridlock had them at a standstill, and Brea began to reflect on her life and her future with Josh. She was in a good place—even though she had only known Josh a short period of time, she felt that she had the balance and stability she lacked as a child growing up in Brooklyn. She felt Josh was her *soulmate*, and she was now starting to find peace with her decision to marry him.

51

West Memphis was still exactly the way he remembered it. Mitch knew a guy from Orange Mound when he attended Texas Southern and wondered what became of the guy, but this wasn't a social visit. He stopped in Memphis because he was simply tired of driving and needed to get some sleep.

He had rushed back to his hotel room and grabbed all his belongings after he pulled the gun on Norris at the club. He left Chicago with no plans of returning anytime in the immediate future as he embarked on his journey to Baton Rouge in search of Max. He had no strategy to bring him down—all he wanted was a face-to-face meeting with him. Let the chips fall where they may.

He got himself a room at a cheap motel at about nine in the morning because he hadn't slept since Sunday. All he remembered was his face hitting the pillow, and when he awakened, darkness was setting in. His watch read six fifteen, and he was starving.

Once he sat up on his bed, he realized he had once again fallen asleep with his clothes on. He outstretched his arms and went to the bathroom to relieve his bladder. He was upset with himself for oversleeping because his original plan was to sleep for a few hours and be in Baton Rouge by nightfall.

He decided to grab something to eat before hitting the road again once he freshened up, and he remembered seeing a Popeye's Chicken a mile in the opposite direction right off Interstate 55. He got dressed after he took a shower and took five crisp one-hundred-dollar bills from his stash that was tucked deep inside his main suitcase. The twenty bundles of one-hundred-dollar bills were the only remnants of the life he once enjoyed, and the money that he had extracted from his safe was the only thing the IRS wasn't able to take from him other than his stocks and bonds in his mother's name.

He grabbed his luggage, paid the clerk at the front desk, and took off. It was almost as cold in Memphis as it was in Chicago but not cold enough to snow. He left the parking lot without letting the car warm up, and he was at Popeye's a few minutes later. The cashier inside was a cutie with an hourglass figure, but her gold front tooth completely threw him off when she smiled at him. She had a striking resemblance to Brea, and the only differences between them were that she was a couple of inches shorter than Brea, and of course, the gold tooth.

"Welcome to Popeye's. How can I help you?" the cashier asked with a southern drawl.

"Let me get a three-piece white," Mitch answered.

"What's your side?"

"I'll have some coleslaw."

"That will be $4.31."

Mitch handed her a hundred-dollar bill, and the cashier asked, "Damn, big baller, don't you have anything smaller?"

"Sorry, I don't," he answered.

"Well, we're not allowed to take anything more than a twenty at night."

"No problem," Mitch said. "I'll be right back...I should've filled up at the gas station first."

"Okay, we'll be here," she said. "I'll keep it nice and hot for you."

Mitch smiled at her, and she returned his smile with a flirtatious smile of her own. He shook his head and exited the restaurant, and he observed a Shell a half-block down the road. It took forty dollars and fifteen cents to fill up his tank, so he went back inside to get his change from the fifty dollars he paid the clerk once he was done pumping gas.

He rushed back to Popeye's, only to find a long line that was almost out the door. He also noticed that his new friend wasn't at the register anymore. If he weren't so hungry, he would've definitely looked for somewhere else to eat instead of waiting in line.

He finally got to order his food after a ten-minute wait, but the second cashier wasn't nearly as friendly. She seemed to have a slight attitude—like the job was beneath her or something.

"May I help you?" she asked after she sighed.

"Uh, let me get a three-piece white with coleslaw," Mitch answered.

"We're all out of white meat," she said. "We have legs and thighs only."

"I was just here, and there were plenty of breasts and wings," he said. "Can you drop some more?"

"Yeah, but it's gonna be a fifteen-minute wait," she answered.

"That's okay, never mind," Mitch said, and he got out of line and left.

He got into his car slightly irritated, and he was on the interstate in less than a minute in search of another fast food restaurant. There was a car stalled a mile down the road with its hazard lights flashing, so he decided to be a good Samaritan and pull over behind the disabled auto. He was at constant war with who he used to be and who he had become in the last few weeks, but the angel had won over the demon in that particular instance. He noticed that it was the girl from Popeye's inside the car when he walked up to the driver's side door.

She rolled down her window and said, "Thanks for stopping. I was afraid I was gonna be stuck out here all night long."

"No problem," he said. "What's wrong with your car?"

"I don't know...it just died on me in the middle of the road. I'm lucky I was able to pull over to the side without getting hit by another car."

"Did you run out of gas?"

"No, I just filled up this afternoon."

"Come on. I'll give you a ride wherever you need to go. I'm Mitch by the way."

"And I'm Desiree," she said while shaking his hand. "Nice to meet you."

"So, where can I take you?" he asked as he opened the passenger side door for her.

"My dorm room, please. I go to Memphis State."

"I know where it is—I went to some wild parties there back in the day."

"You went to Memphis State?"

"Nah, I went to Texas Southern. I had a frat brother who was from here, and we went to a few Kappa parties at Memphis State whenever we were in town."

"You pledged Kappa?"

Mitch sighed and said, "Yes, in another life, I did."

"You sound like you regret it."

"I had a lot of fun—maybe too much fun, but I don't regret or miss anything about the Greek life."

"I see. So, where are you from?"

"I'm from Chicago."

"You're here to visit your frat brother, huh?"

"Nope, I'm just passing through."

"Well, I'm glad you are."

He merged onto the highway from the shoulder once he saw an opening. Moments later, she glanced over at him for a second once she noticed that he was smiling at her.

"What?" she asked abruptly. "Is something funny?"

"I'm sorry," he replied. "It's just that you look like someone I used to know."

"Is that good or bad?"

"It's good and bad—you look just like my ex-girlfriend."

"Well, she must be fine as hell," she said in a sassy tone.

"She was," he laughed. "I mean, she is."

"Why did you two break up?"

"To make a long story short, she cheated on me."

"I'm sorry to hear that."

"Don't be—breaking up with her was for the best."

They continued their conversation—well, she did most of the talking. She talked about school and her job mostly, and he listened attentively in spite of the fact that he wasn't really in a talkative mood. Time seemed to pass rather swiftly, and they were on campus before they realized it. There were a few students walking around when they arrived at her dormitory, but for the most part, it was quiet.

He pulled out his phone from his pocket and asked, "Do you need me to call a tow truck for your car?"

"Uh, I don't know who to call..."

"Relax, I have AAA Motor Club. I can call them, and they should be able to tow your car in about an hour."

"Thank you so much, Mitch. I don't know what I would've done if you hadn't shown up when you did."

"I'm glad I could help."

"Wanna come inside my dorm to wait for them to show up?"

"Nah, you go ahead. I'm gonna take off after I make this call, and here's one hundred dollars—I'll have them tow your car back to the dorm from the highway."

"Okay, thanks, Mitch. Wanna hang out tomorrow? I only have one class in the morning..."

"I'm afraid not, Desiree."

"Why? What's your rush?"

"Like I said, I'm just passing through."

"I understand. I was just hoping to see you again; that's all."

"Look, I think you're beautiful, but we probably won't see each other again because I don't plan on ever coming back here."

"Never say never, Mitch. Besides, who knows what the future holds?"

"God only knows, but that's another subject. It was nice meeting you, though."

"Likewise. Let me get your address and phone number so that I can send you the money."

"Don't worry about the money. You don't have to pay me back."

"Thank you, baby."

"You're welcome."

"Well, can we at least exchange phone numbers? If I'm ever in Chicago, I'll look you up."

"Okay, I don't see the harm in that."

Desiree dialed Mitch's number and programmed it in her phone, and he saved her's in his phone. They embraced, and she kissed him on the cheek.

"Take care of yourself," he said. "Maybe I'll see you on my way back."

"Back from where?" she asked.

"Baton Rouge. I'm going to visit an old friend of mine."

"That's great. I can't wait to see you again."

"Goodbye, Desiree."

"Bye, Mitch."

He waved at her and slowly drove off. She continued to stand in the middle of the street watching his taillights disappear into the darkness. He immediately shifted his focus on Max—he contemplated shooting him on sight or making him beg for mercy before putting his lights out for good. He figured a quick death without torturing him was too easy, but he also wanted to make sure he avenged Wesley's death properly.

He subsequently shifted his thoughts to his encounter with Desiree—and like his experience with Natalie—he had no real interest in getting to know her better, either. However, he kept her number programmed in his phone and didn't want to rule out the possibility of making a genuine friend because good friends were hard to come by, and nobody knew that better than he did.

52

She angrily glared at him while she changed their infant daughter's diaper. He was slouching on their living room couch sipping on a Pepsi and watching the Cleveland Cavaliers play the Golden State Warriors on local television. Tisha threw the soiled diaper and baby wipe in the trash can and said, "Can-you-please take out the garbage?"

"Alright, I'll do at halftime," Jimmy replied.

"That damn game can wait, Jimmy."

"Damn, Tisha, why you bothering me?"

"Because you never help me out. I didn't make this baby by myself."

"Okay, I'll do it in a minute."

"You know what, I'm outta here. You can watch your daughter by yourself for the rest of the evening."

"I have a test tomorrow, so I have to study."

"Not my problem, Jimmy."

Tisha was out the door and in her car before Jimmy could say another word. Tameka was wide-eyed and smiling at her dad while secured in her high chair a few feet from the television. He shook his head and whisked baby Tameka into his arms and kissed her on the forehead. She giggled when Jimmy rubbed noses with her.

Tisha was on Scenic Highway en route to Harding Boulevard, and then she was on the way to Interstate 110 heading southbound in the direction of New Orleans several minutes later. She smiled devilishly as she readjusted her rearview mirror.

"That was easier than I thought it was gonna be," Tisha said to herself. She dialed Max's number, and he picked up on the third ring.

"Hello?" Max asked.

"Hey, baby, it's me," Tisha answered. "Are you there yet?"

"Nah, I'm just leaving the shop. I'm on my way."

"Okay, I'll see you in a few minutes."

She was going to meet him at the Days Inn off Siegan Lane. This was their first rendezvous, and she wanted everything to be perfect. She had cheated on Jimmy one other time with one of his teammates because he cheated on her with a cheerleader first, but Max was special. She was completed infatuated with him and was determined to have him all to herself one day, even if it meant losing her newfound friendship with Jill.

Since Max was running behind, Tisha decided to stop at the liquor store to buy some wine for herself and some beer for Max. She also bought a pack of condoms just in case he didn't come prepared.

She arrived at the Days Inn parking lot and waited. He showed up not long afterwards.

"Hey, baby," Tisha said with outstretched arms.

"Hey," Max said, giving her a kiss and a tight embrace. "Do you have a credit card? Because I can give you the cash right now..."

"Sure, sweetheart, no problem," she answered. "You must really have it going on because all I see you do is pay cash for everything."

"Nah, I wouldn't say all that. I wasn't always a barber, you know."

"Oh really? So, what were you into back in Chi-town, Mr. Maxwell?"

"Let's just say I was into a lot of different stuff back then, but I've straightened out my life for my son."

"I'm not judging you because I'm no angel, either."

"Anyway, let's get this room, ma."

Max grabbed the bag on the passenger side seat. They went to the lobby to get the room, and it was conveniently on the side where they both parked. Once they got inside, Max grabbed Tisha's waist and pulled her toward him for a passionate kiss. He let go his embrace and sat on the bed a minute or so later. She sat down next to him and placed her hand over his.

"I can't even believe I'm doing this," Max said. "I still don't know what I'm gonna tell Jill."

"Relax, Max," Tisha said. "You're worrying for no reason. Just tell her you went out for some drinks with the guys from the shop.

Don't even sweat this—I promise I'll have you back home before it gets too late."

"What about the room?"

"I'll come back up here and check us out before I go to class tomorrow. I got everything under control."

"Well, all right then. I guess you done this type of thing before, huh?"

"So, what are you saying?"

"I'm not trying to imply anything—it's just that your street game is kinda tight for a country girl."

"I'll take that as a compliment, I guess. I'm originally from Chicago, though."

"That explains it."

Max paused and said, "So, what's up with you and Jimmy? I thought y'all really loved each other."

"I could say the same thing about you and Jill, but I'm not gonna go there."

"Me and Jill are fine, Tisha," he said, looking down at the carpet, "but there's definitely something between *us*. I woke up this morning thinking about what we did yesterday."

"I've wanted you since the first time I saw you, Max."

She leaned in and kissed him softly on his lips. He loved the way her cherry lip gloss tasted, and the scent of her perfume turned him on even more. They both fell back on the bed, and he lay on top of her as their kisses became deeper and more sensual. He worked his way to her neck and then to her chest; he removed her tube-top, daisy dukes, and panties before completely disrobing himself.

Her smooth, caramel complexion was impeccable, and he resumed exploring every inch of her beautiful body. He took his time and made sure she was completely satisfied before reaching his own level of utopia—mastering the art of figuring out what pleased her sexually and putting it into action. They completely lost the concept of time as the clock read ten o'clock. He then held her in his arms completely exhausted from several rounds of intense lovemaking.

"We never got around to drinking the liquor you bought," Max said. "Once we got started, I couldn't help myself."

"I knew you'd be good," Tisha said. "I can honestly say that no guy has ever worked me over the way you just did in my young life, Max."

"I aim to please, but we have to keep this on the low."

"I agree. Too many people would be affected by our affair coming to light. We have to cover our tracks."

He got up from the bed and grabbed a beer out of the mini fridge, and he got the bottle of Gancia Asti out of the fridge and poured her a glass. He handed her the glass of wine and sat next to her on the bed.

"Thank you, baby," she said. "I love drinking this after a hard day's work."

"You're welcome," he said. "I usually wind down with a beer."

"You are such a gentleman, Max. I never would have guess that in a million years."

"Why do you say that?"

"You seem like the roughneck type to me."

"I am the roughneck type, but I still know how to treat a woman. I have five sisters, so knowing how a woman thinks came naturally to me."

"Jimmy could take notes from a guy like you."

"I don't want to talk about Jimmy or Jill. All I wanna do is focus on you right now."

He kissed her gently, and he put his arms around her and said, "I really like you, Tisha."

"I feel the same way you do, and I want to take things to the next level, Max."

Max's cell phone rang suddenly, and it startled both of them. He answered it on the first ring.

"What's up, Mack?" Max asked.

"Where you at, dawg?" Tyrone asked.

"I'm just hanging out. Why?"

"I thought we were gonna handle this situation tonight."

"Damn , I forgot, man. Where are you?"

"I'm parked in front of these fools' crib. How fast can you get here?"

"I'll meet you in about fifteen minutes."

"Aiight, later."

"Who was that?" Tisha asked.

"That was Tyrone, babe," Max answered. "I gotta go handle some business."

"Oh, okay. Call me later?"

"Okay," he said after quickly putting on his clothes. "I'll call you later."

He hastened out of the motel room, hopped in his blue Dodge Durango truck, and quickly sped off as he exited the parking lot. He reached in his glove compartment, and he pulled out his .380 and said to himself, "Time to teach these dudes a lesson."

53

The melodic music was pulsating through the mammoth speakers stationed throughout the club. The DJ on the wheels of steel had introduced the crowd to Future's new track, and the crowd went crazy. The Jones twins were on the dance floor doing their thing, and Josh and his brother Steve were drinking tequila shots at the bar. His other brother Joseph and his sister Brittany couldn't make the trip because of their jobs, so it was just the four of them along with some friends that night.

DJ Uptown worked the crowd with a few more underground tracks before he blended in Brea's new single "You Shoud've Loved Me Better". She stopped dancing and was completely flabbergasted.

"Yo, sis, that's your joint, ain't it?" Bria asked. "That sounds fresh as hell."

"Oh my God!" Brea shouted excitedly. "That's my song!"

The crowd erupted and started chanting Brea's name. Josh and Steve had busted through the crowd, and Josh lifted Brea off the floor with a tight embrace.

"Your song is the bomb, baby," Josh said. "You're about to blow up."

"Yeah, Brea, congratulations," Steve said.

"Thanks, guys. I'm so psyched that I can hardly breathe," Brea said.

Brea continued to receive well wishes and even signed a few autographs while Bria stood by her side. However, Josh and Steve had disappeared and were gone quite a while. Brea began searching for Josh throughout the club, once she was done being a celebrity for the moment, but couldn't locate him, while Bria started dancing with a guy in the middle of the floor.

She wondered if Josh and his brother went outside, but she figured Josh would've said something if he decided to leave the club. She decided to check the men's bathroom where anything and everything goes. She entered the restroom and saw a girl giving a guy oral sex in the first stall. She wasn't all that surprised because she'd witnessed that type of stuff all the time when she was a stripper back in the day. She looked straight ahead as men and women were smoking cigarettes and conversing, and it was then she noticed Josh and Steve doing cocaine lines on the sink in the back of the bathroom.

"What the hell are you doing, Josh?" Brea asked.

"Uh, nothing, baby," Josh answered, caught off-guard. "We're just partying—don't worry. It ain't that deep."

"If it ain't that deep, why are you keeping it a secret?"

"I was gonna tell you," Josh answered, "but I just couldn't find the right time..."

"Take a chill pill, Brea," Steve interjected. "It's not like we do this all the time. We only do it on special occasions like this."

"Well, that explains what I saw on the kitchen counter," Brea said. "You were quick to clean it up, weren't you?"

"No, sweetheart, that was chicken flour," Josh pleaded. "I don't have a cocaine habit."

"I really love you, Josh, but I can't do this," Brea said. "I lost both of my parents because of drugs, and I won't go through that ever again."

"Brea, wait," Josh said.

"Goodbye, Josh," Brea said.

She pulled her engagement ring off her finger and placed it forcefully in Josh's hand, and she abruptly walked out of the bathroom. She spotted Bria on the dance floor and shouted out her name.

"Bria!" she shouted. "Let's get outta here!"

"What's wrong, sis?" Bria asked. "You're gonna leave your own engagement party?"

"Yes, and I'll tell you everything once we get outside," Brea replied. "Come on."

Bria followed Brea to the front entrance of the club and outside to the parking lot. Bria's rental car was in a parking space at the front of the lot.

"What happened?" Bria asked.

"Josh and his brother were doing lines in the men's bathroom," Brea replied. "It's over."

"Just like that?"

"Yeah, just like that. I can't mess with a guy who uses drugs—I don't care if he's an addict or not."

"I understand where you coming from, and I'm here for you, Brea. I mean it."

"Thank you, Bria. Let's just go."

"Okay."

They left the club and rushed back to Josh's place to get her things. She never got around to getting the bulk of her belongings out of storage in Chicago, so all that she had was a couple of suitcases.

They rode in silence the entire way, and all Brea could do was stare out the passenger side window. Tears cascaded down her face like a waterfall, and her heart was completely shattered. Karma quickly came around, and she now understood completely how Mitch felt when she broke it off with him.

54

Max and Tyrone were casing out Piru's house about a half-mile from the Southern University campus in Tyrone's Chevy Impala after Max parked his truck on the opposite side of the street a few spaces back. Piru and his cronies had the entire spot humming as people were lined up halfway down the block waiting for the candy store to open. They really didn't have a concrete plan to bum rush their spot and waste all three of them, so Max lit a cigarette while he contemplated their next move.

Max and Tyrone had been partners in crime for nearly a decade. They met in Chicago shortly after Max got kicked out of Texas Southern for selling weed. Max had a cousin who stayed in Harvey, Illinois, so he crashed there until he could figure out his plans for the future. It turned out that Tyrone was his cousin's good friend, and Tyrone and Max had become instant best friends since then.

"What's the plan, Max?" Tyrone asked.

"I still trying to figure that out, Mack," Max answered. "I think the element of surprise is key in this situation because we're outnumbered."

"No doubt. We should wait until this line dies down before we make our move on these rookies."

"Nah, I think now is the perfect time to pounce on them. See that over there—Spider is too busy servin' those weed heads to be paying any attention to us."

"Yeah, let's take him out."

"Nah, wait..."

"What?"

"I got a better idea. We can get the police to bust this party up."

"You wanna snitch on them?"

"We're business owners now, Mack. We have everything to lose if we kill them, and I don't want us to go out like that."

"You going soft on me, Max—this is not how we do things."

"You know there's nothing soft about me—I got a son to raise, and he's not gonna grow up without a father like we did, man."

"You know I'm with you either way. I got your back."

"I appreciate that. Now, let's eliminate this problem for good."

Max dialed 911 and let the operator know that Piru and his crew were dealing on Snipe Street a block away from Scenic Drive. Max's house was just a quarter mile away from Piru's house on Snipe Street. There were literally cops on the scene before Max could hang up his phone.

"Damn, they must have already been in the area," Tyrone said.

"Yeah, it kinda makes you wonder though," Max said. "Did the police know they were servin' all along?"

"Maybe, but what if they could never make a bust before tonight?"

"Well, they haven't been in the game that long, and it shows. They're sloppy as hell."

Several minutes later, more police cars and a paddy wagon parked in the middle of the street, and numerous arrests were made. They watched the whole thing unfold a half-block down. Piru, Spider, and Bam were brought out in handcuffs, along with some of their customers.

"Hopefully, we won't have to deal with these fools no more," Max said. "They have been a nuisance ever since we got here."

"Yeah, they won't see the light of day for a long time with the amount of weight they had in their crib, I bet," Tyrone added.

Tyrone paused and said, "Yo, where were you earlier? I called you three times before you finally picked up."

"I lied..."

"Lied about what?"

"About being with Tisha."

"Yeah? Are you hittin' that?"

"Yeah, once, but I'm trying to keep it on the low."

"Damn, man, you slippin'."

"Don't worry, I got everything under control. I'm not gonna risk losing Jill or my son."

"I hope you do have everything under control for your sake, homeboy."

"I tried to fight her off, but she wore me down. The sex was good, too, bruh."

"Now I know you slippin'—so—what you gonna do about it?"

"I don't know. I like Jimmy, and I hate doing this behind his back."

"You done lost your damn mind."

"She might be a problem, though. She said she wants to take things to the next level, so I might have to cut her loose."

"This is gonna cause friction inside the clique."

"It'll just have to be the four of us like before. Tisha is just Jill's nail technician—she can find somebody else."

"I feel you, bruh."

"Come on. Let's get outta here."

Tyrone waited until the last police car drove off, and then Max motioned to get out of Tyrone's car but paused.

"Yo, I need to take a shower at your crib to get this sex off me," Max said.

"No problem. How long have you been messing with her?"

"Since yesterday—we made out in the parking lot."

"No wonder y'all took so long. You don't think Jill suspects anything, do you?"

"Nah, I still had enough in the tank to wear her out last night, but I don't have nothing in the tank tonight."

"I hope you can keep this up because the moment you start neglecting Jill, all hell is gonna break loose."

"That's not gonna happen, man. Tisha has just as much to lose as I do, so relax."

"Okay, but it's your funeral."

"Mack, you need to worry about your own relationship—dudes be trying to get at Melissa seven days a week."

"Me and Mel are good, bro. Them college dudes ain't got nothing on your boy."

"Aiight, Romeo, you know what you're doing. I'mma stay outta it."

"I appreciate your concern just like I know you appreciate mine."

"No doubt, Mack."

55

Mitch entered the Louisiana state line blurry-eyed and exhausted well over an hour ago and was heading due west on Interstate 12 to Baton Rouge. He had decided to get off at the Denham Springs exit to get some gas and coffee before he found a motel room. He was going to peruse the Southern campus later that morning to find Max and deal with the fallout afterwards.

He spotted a Chevron gas station a few blocks off the highway and pulled up to a pump. He then went inside the convenient store and was taken aback when he saw who was behind the cash register.

"Yo, is that you, Tommy?" Mitch asked.

"Mitch?" Tommy G asked. "What's up, kid?"

They gave each other dap, and Mitch said, "Man, I haven't seen you since high school. How's everything going?"

"Everything is copacetic, homeboy. What about you?"

"I can't complain. I'm tired as hell, though."

"So, what brings you down here?"

"It's a long story, man. Lemme get a cup of coffee, and I'll tell you all about it."

"Sure, no problem. I'm about to get off in a few minutes, so we can sit at one of the booths and catch up."

Mitch paid Tommy G for his coffee and fill up, and Mitch pumped his gas while Tommy and his relief started their shift change process of balancing the cash register. Mitch sipped on his coffee at one of the booths by the window after pumping his gas, and Tommy G was done in about ten minutes.

"I almost didn't recognize you with the beard," Tommy G said. "You're looking good."

"Thanks, man," Mitch said.

"So, what have you been doing with yourself?"

"Well, to make a long story short, I was on top of the world one minute, but I lost everything in less than a year."

"What happened?"

Mitch told Tommy G his sob story about losing his wife, job, most of his material possessions in a span of six months; he also told him about Brea being the catalyst for most of his current plight. Tommy G listened attentively and shared some of his own misfortune. He told Mitch about having to relocate to Baton Rouge, but he wasn't that forthcoming about why he had to leave Chicago. He merely said the Feds were on his tail, and that he was keeping a low profile on his business.

"So lemme get this straight," Tommy G said. "You've been married, got divorced, lost your job, and you ain't even thirty yet. You've lived a full life already."

"I guess you can say that, but that's only part of the story," Mitch said.

"So, there's more?"

"I also owned a nightclub, but the IRS seized it because I owe millions of dollars in back taxes."

"Man, are you serious?"

"I'm dead serious, Tommy. I had the hottest spot in town, but everything fell apart after Wes died."

"Wes is dead?"

"Yeah, he was killed last year. My club got shot up, and he got caught in the crossfire. I was under the radar from the Feds until that happened."

"Damn, I'm sorry to hear that, man. Did they ever catch the dudes that did it?"

"Nah, and that's why I'm down here. I know who did it, and I'm gonna make them pay."

"Word?"

"No doubt. It's a coincidence that I ran into you tonight because I heard all about those guys who shot up your spot last year, too."

"You knew about that?"

"Yeah, it was all over the news, and your uncle told me who was responsible."

"Yeah? But why did he share that with you?"

"Because the same guys who shot up my club are the same guys who killed your whole crew."

"You know who set me up?"

"Yes, that's what I'm trying to tell you. Two guys named Tyrone Mack and Gary Maxwell robbed you and me last year. Gary used to be my roommate and teammate in college, and he killed Wes in cold blood."

"You can do what you want with this Gary dude, but Tyrone is my problem. When do you wanna move on them?"

"Gary owns a barbershop near the Southern campus, so I'm gonna stake out the joint in the morning."

"You mean to tell me that they've been down here the whole time?"

Mitch nodded.

"How come my uncle didn't come after them?"

"He didn't know where they were. Hell, he was supposed to help me find them, but I haven't heard one word from him in over three weeks."

"I haven't talked to him since I fled Chicago. I haven't contacted nobody—no family or friends."

"I know the cops are still looking for you."

"Well, I'm never going back."

There was brief silence, and then Mitch said, "Here's my cell number. Call me first thing in the morning, so we can come up with a game plan. If I know Max, he's definitely strapped and ready for battle."

"Okay, Mitch, I'll talk to you in the morning."

They embraced, and Mitch left the store. He wasted no time jumping back on the highway, and he entered Baton Rouge city limits moments later. He saw a few hotels and motels right off the expressway, so he exited on the first ramp.

He entered the Days Inn parking lot and pulled up in front of the entrance. All his credit cards were frozen because of the audit, but he was somehow able to get a new VISA with a fake social security number. He had used Brea's address initially, but he had since been using the hotel's address where he was staying.

He checked in at the front desk and got his room key. The only thing on his mind was lying down on a soft, king size bed and relaxing. He was tired but not too sleepy because he had slept until earlier that evening. As he was parking his car, he made eye contact with a caramel beauty who had the most captivating smile he had seen since his ex-wife.

He got out of his car and stared—trying not to gawk at her but couldn't completely compose himself. However, he soon realized the caramel beauty was his cousin Tisha and felt slightly embarrassed. She was about to leave the hotel for home after cleaning herself up from frolicking around with Max. Luckily, it appeared she didn't notice his horns showing for that brief moment. Her smile widened once she realized who he was, and she walked toward him.

"Oh my god," she shouted, hugging him tightly, "how have you been?"

"I've been okay, Tish," he said. "Just taking it day by day. How about you?"

"I've been good. How's everybody?"

"Everybody's good. Nana asked me about you last month."

"I miss everybody so much, Mitch, and I'm sorry I couldn't make it to Wesley's funeral. I just had my daughter Tameka and couldn't travel."

"Don't even sweat that. I totally understand."

"I know how close you two were. I loved him too, and I think about him a lot."

"I didn't even know you were down here—it's been so long since we seen each other. I almost didn't recognize you."

"I know because you were practically undressing me with your eyes."

"No, I wasn't," he laughed, "but it's still good to see you. Does auntie ever visit you down here?"

"Nah, Momma's never leaving St. Louis. She says the drive is too long, and she's still afraid of flying. I'm surprised that she even went to the funeral last year."

"Yeah, me, too. That was only the second time she came to Chicago since you all moved."

"So, cuz, what brings you to Baton Rouge?"

"It's a long story—maybe we can catch up tomorrow. Are you free?"

"Yeah, but it will have to be in the evening. I have class in the morning, and I have to work until five."

"Oh, okay. So, what are doing at a motel in the wee hours of the morning?"

"That's also a long story, and I'll tell you all about it when we hang out."

"Fair enough. Where do you go to school?"

"I go to Southern, and my major is computer science."

"That's great. I majored in finance at Texas Southern."

"I remember you telling me that—Texas Southern was one of my choices."

"Girl, you're all grown up now. The last time I saw you, you were a skinny sixteen-year-old with braces."

"That's right—now I'm a grown woman with some grown-woman issues."

"Damn, I can definitely relate to that."

Mitch paused and said, "That's a dope ride you got. Is that a 2018 BMW?"

"Yeah, you know your girl gotta be the freshest one out here."

"That's what's up, Tish. What you do to pay the bills?"

"I do nails at a salon a few blocks from campus, and I still have a good portion of my trust fund my father set up for me."

"How's Uncle George doing?"

"I don't know. I haven't gone to the prison to see him since I graduated high school."

She paused after her last comment and said, "You should let me hook you up with a manicure."

"Nah, I'll pass on that, but I'll treat you to some hot wings at Hooters tomorrow if you want."

"You have yourself a date. Here's my number, and I'll see you tomorrow at about six, okay?"

"Sounds great. Bye, Tish."

Tisha handed Mitch her business card with her address and phone number on it. He had her program his phone number in her cell, and they embraced again. He watched her walk to her car and drive off in her sleek, black BMW with twenty-inch chrome rims. He then went inside his room, which happened to be two doors down from hers at Room 219. Mitch lay on the bed and was out for the count not long afterwards.

Tisha had made up her mind that she was going to live life to the fullest with no regrets. She had to find a way to end things with Jimmy because she felt that the relationship had run its full course. She wasn't in love with him anymore, even though she still cared for him, and she wanted to start a new life with the possibility of Max in it. Unfortunately, Jill was the only obstacle standing in her way to complete happiness. She was going to end things with Jimmy after her morning classes, and there was no turning back.

56

It was a brisk, cool Tuesday morning as the sun crept in and out of the clouds. A couple of crows circled some trash that overflowed from the garbage can in front of the barbershop. Tommy G sat in his rusty, sky blue Chevy Impala and waited. There were a few students who walked to and fro the campus, and the shop hadn't opened yet.

Max's Dodge Durango suddenly parked in front of the entrance, and Max and Tyrone got out. Max unlocked the front door, and they went inside. There weren't any customers waiting, so Tommy G saw that as the perfect opportunity to take out both of them. He hopped out of his car, pulled the hood of his sweatshirt over his head, and trotted to the front door. He eased his gun out of his jeans and stormed inside.

"Remember me, Mack?" Tommy G asked with his gun cocked. "Get ready to die!"

"Get down, Max!" Tyrone shouted, reaching for his gun.

Tyrone was too late with his draw, and Tommy G let off two shots before Max blasted Tommy G's center mass. Both Tyrone and Tommy G fell to the floor, and Tommy G's body started convulsing. Tyrone appeared to be okay with just a flesh wound to his left shoulder. Max checked Tommy G's pulse, but he was dead.

"You aiight?" Max asked.

"Yeah, but it burns like hell," Tyrone answered. "Is he dead?"

"Yeah, he's lights out. Who the hell is he?"

"That—was Tommy G."

"That's the dude we robbed last year?"

"Yep, that's the no-good coward that left his crew for dead. He didn't deserve to live."

"Damn, how did he find out where we were?"

"Good question, but we have to dump his body."

"Lemme see your shoulder..."

"I'm good...just get me one of those towels in the back."

Max scurried to the back of the shop and got a towel for Tyrone. He peeked outside to see if anyone was around, and there were two guys standing at the end of the block trying to pinpoint the location of the gunshots.

"We got a small window to get rid of the body," Max said. "I'mma pull the truck around the back."

"Okay."

Max calmly strolled outside to his truck and drove it to the back of the shop. The guys on the corner were now walking toward the campus, and he parked the truck in the middle of the alley. He looked both ways, he left the passenger side back door open, and he rushed inside. They then got two 30-gallon trash bags and quickly placed them over Bobby's head and feet, and they used duct tape to secure the two bags around his waist.

"Let's put him inside the truck," Max instructed.

They picked up Tommy G's lifeless body and tossed it in the back seat. Luckily, he was a skinny guy, who barely weighed one hundred fifty pounds. They then looked both ways down the alley and saw the coast was clear. Max rushed back inside to wipe up any traces of blood on the floor with a damp towel before locking the front door. He placed the towel in a plastic bag and took it with him once he exited the back entrance.

"Where are we gonna dump him?" Tyrone asked.

"Let's dump him somewhere in Lake Pontchartrain," Max replied. "Hopefully, the alligators will get to him before the cops do."

"Man, I thought I was a goner. That fool couldn't shoot worth a damn."

"Yeah, lucky for you he couldn't."

"Good looking out, though."

"I got your back, Mack."

57

Mitch was watching the eleven o'clock news while drinking his morning coffee. He waited patiently for Tommy G's call—a call he never received. He got dressed and left to go find Max after the news went off. He saw that the shop was crowded once he arrived, and that was clearly not a good sign. He knew the shop belonged to Max because of the name—*Tailor Made Cuts*. It was the same name he used when they were at Texas Southern.

He parked his car and waited.

"What was I going to say to him?" he asked himself.

The meeting between Max and him was about to take place, and his excitement began to overtake him. His heart was pounding, but it wasn't out of fear. He dreamt about killing Max for weeks, and he was ready to blast everyone in the barbershop if provoked to do so.

However, he was able to calm himself down and listen to his inner voice telling him to be smart after about fifteen minutes, and that's when he tucked the Glock inside his jeans and under his Chicago Bulls t-shirt. He then walked up to the shop and went inside. All the seats were filled, and there appeared to be only two barbers on duty. Things seemed to be a little hectic, as there were even a few patrons standing up as they waited to get a haircut. He asked one of the barbers about Max after standing around for what seemed like an eternity.

"Is Max around?" Mitch asked.

"No, he won't be in today," one of the barbers replied. "I'll tell him you were looking for him when he comes back. What's your name, bro?"

"Nah, you don't have to do that," Mitch answered. "I'll just come back tomorrow."

"You sure? Because it's no trouble..."

"Yeah, I'm good," Mitch said. "Thanks."

"No problem," he said.

Mitch left the shop and mulled over his next move as he drove back to the motel. He had a bunch of time to kill before he was going to hang out with Tisha, so he stopped at a liquor store and bought a six pack of Miller Draft.

He knew killing Max wasn't going to bring Wesley back, but he still wanted closure. He thought maybe he should call the police, but he had no physical evidence to tie Max to any of the murders. He finally decided to stay in town an extra day, so he could have his face-to-face meeting with Max. It was time to man up, and he was going to finish what he started no matter what the outcome.

58

"Girl, I am so in love with him that I can hardly see straight," Tisha said to one of her girlfriends. "Can you believe he told me that he felt the same way, too?"

"For real?" she said.

"Please believe me, Yvette," Tisha replied. "And I'm gonna really put it on him when I see him again, but the only problem is his wife, Jill."

"But I thought you and Jill were friends."

"We are, but I can't help the way I feel about Max."

"You better slow down before you get caught up," Yvette said. "Jimmy don't play that."

"The hell with Jimmy. I'm leaving him today."

"Are you sure you wanna do that?"

"I'm absolutely positive. I just wanna be free to do what I want, when I want."

"You're gonna kick him out?"

"Yeah, he can move back into the dorm with the basketball team. I can raise Tameka by myself—hell, I'm doing it mostly by myself anyway."

"I don't know, Tisha. Jimmy's a good man..."

"I don't love him anymore, Yvette."

"Okay, I hear you. What you do is your business."

"I know it is."

"Well, I'll see you in class tomorrow."

"Alright, I'll holla at you later."

Tisha walked toward the parking lot to get her car, and then it was off to the house before going to the beauty shop. She had four hours to put in and five clients scheduled, but first she had to deal with Jimmy. She called him earlier and told him they needed to talk. She could hear the apprehension in his voice, but that wasn't going to stop her from going for the jugular. She was fed up, and she was dying to let him know how she really felt.

She arrived at their apartment, and Jimmy was already there. Tameka was in daycare, so this was her opportunity to lay into him. He was sitting on the living room couch in deep thought with no television or radio on.

"So, what you want to talk about, Tisha?" he asked with dejection in his voice.

She sat down on the other side of the sofa and replied, "It's over, Jimmy. I want you to pack up your things and move out today."

"What did I do?" he asked, tears beginning to stream down his face. "I don't wanna lose you, baby. I love you."

"Stop crying, Jimmy. You're a pathetic excuse for a man, and I'm tired of this relationship."

"I can fix this if you just give me a chance."

"I've given you numerous chances, but the fact of the matter is I don't love you anymore."

"Wait, baby, we can fix this..."

"I'm sorry, Jimmy, but this can't be fixed. I want you gone by the time I get back. You can see Tameka anytime you want, and in spite of the fact that you've done a poor job of taking care of my needs, you're a good father. I won't deny you seeing your daughter."

"I'm begging you, Tisha—please don't do this."

"Goodbye, Jimmy."

He buried his face in his hands and never looked up once Tisha stormed out the apartment. She felt guilty and sad for him, but a small part of her felt relieved. "Now I can have the life I've always wanted without being tied down to him," she said to herself.

She strolled to her car and belted out a sigh of relief, hopped in and sat there for a minute to collect her thoughts. She looked back at the house one more time, and she put on her Chanel glasses before driving off.

59

Tyrone had just made it back to the barbershop after he and Max dumped Tommy G's body in the lake. Max, on the other hand, had some business at home that he needed to handle and couldn't make it to the shop. The spot had been busy all day, and Tyrone was there to help with the crowd. Normally, the five of them—Max, Paul, Mark, Sly, and Tyrone—served the customers like a well-oiled machine. However, Sly had the day off, and Paul and Mark had to fend for themselves for the greater part of the day. They were also able to function well even with only three barbers, but trying to operate with only two barbers on a busy Tuesday was a virtual nightmare.

The three of them humped until closing time, and a rocky start culminated with each and every patron being satisfied and serviced in a timely fashion. Tyrone let Paul and Mark leave after the last customer, and he cleaned up before closing shop.

Tyrone stepped outside to lock up the shop after sweeping up the hair and taking out the trash, and the plan was to spend time with Melissa for the rest of the night. They were supposed to catch a movie and have dinner.

A black Lincoln town car suddenly pulled up in front of the shop, and the right-side front and rear door flung open. Two men jumped out and forced him back inside. One of the men punched Tyrone in the jaw and knocked him to the floor, and the other guy placed his foot on his neck with his nine-millimeter and silencer aimed at his head. Cedric entered the shop soon after Tyrone got cold-cocked.

"Damn, looks like you got knocked the hell out," Cedric said smugly. "You had to know that I was gonna find you one day."

"Tommy told you where we were, didn't he?"

"No, I'm afraid your cousin Norris ratted you all out before I shot him in the head. What does Tommy have to do with anything?"

"Nothing now because he's swimming with the fishes in Lake Pontchartrain."

"That's real funny, Big Ty. I guess you're going to be joining him real soon."

"Whatever, man," Tyrone said. "If you're gonna kill me, get it over with."

"Don't worry. I'm gonna give you exactly what you want, but first, you're going to tell me where Max is."

"I'm not telling you nothing, homie. If you want your money back, get it from your mama on the corner."

"This isn't about the money, man. It's about respect. You all disrespected me and my business, and I don't tolerate disrespect on any level."

Cedric nodded at his henchman with his foot on Tyrone's neck, and he shot Tyrone in the kneecap.

"Awwwww!" Tyrone bellowed. "Please, just kill me, Cedric!"

"I'm going to ask you one more time," Cedric urged. "Where the hell is Max?"

"I ain't telling you nothing, man..."

Cedric's goon didn't hesitate to riddle Tyrone's body with bullets until his body oozed blood on the black and white checkered floor. Cedric and his men scoured the entire shop for Max's address or phone number.

"Tear this place up if you have to," Cedric instructed. "Williams, call information and see if they have a listing for him."

"Okay, boss," Williams said.

"Stevens, check the office for any info on this prick," Cedric ordered.

"I'm on it," Stevens said.

"I'm not leaving until we find him and stop his clock."

60

"What's going on with you, Gary?" Jill asked. "You've been acting real funny lately."

"I don't know what you're talking about," Max answered. "I can easily say the same thing about you."

"Don't try to turn this around on me," she said, turning completely around to face him from the kitchen. "You haven't paid me any attention in the last couple of weeks, and I want to know why."

"You're tripping, babe. I'm the same I've always been. Quit trying to make something outta nothing."

"I've been with you for ten years, and I know when you're holding something back from me."

"Okay but promise me that you're not gonna worry."

"Worry about what? If you can't tell me what's going on, what are we doing this for?"

Max sat down on the living room sofa and turned off the television. Jill sat next to him and looked him directly in the eyes.

"Tell me what's going on," she said.

"Tommy came to the shop this morning to kill me and Mack."

"Tommy? Who the hell is Tommy?"

"The guy we robbed last summer right off South Shore Drive. Tommy shot Mack, and I killed Tommy today."

"You did what you had to do. Chalk it up to the game."

Jill paused and said, "Is Tyrone okay?"

"Yeah, it was just a flesh wound," Max answered.

"What did you do with the body?"

"We had to dump him in the lake."

"What are we gonna do now?"

"I don't know—we might have to leave Baton Rouge for good."

"Where will we go?"

"Back home to Houston."

"Is something going on with you and Tisha?" Jill asked, changing the subject.

"Why do you ask me that?" he asked

"Just answer the question, Gary. I've got eyes, and I see the way she looks at you."

Max paused and said, "Yeah, I messed up, but it was only one time."

"Don't I turn you on anymore?" Jill asked, tears streaming down her cheeks.

"Of course you do, baby, and I'm sorry. It will never happen again."

"It's my fault for bring her around everybody..."

"No, it's on me, Jill. I'll end things with her tonight."

"No, I'll handle it. I'm not going to lose my family because of this little tramp."

Jill left the house abruptly and drove off to confront Tisha. Max pulled his cigarettes from his pocket and lit one. He suddenly heard a loud knock on the door about five minutes later and got up to answer it.

"Did you forget your keys or something, Jill?" he asked.

Max opened the door, and the last thing Max saw before he was knocked out cold was a massive fist hitting the left side of his jaw.

61

Mitch was waiting patiently for Tisha to show up at Hooters. They hadn't seen each other since the family reunion four years prior, and they had a lot of catching up to do. He looked at his watch, and it read fourteen minutes after six. Tisha walked in shortly afterwards, and Mitch greeted her with a hug.

"Sorry I'm late," Tisha said. "I had to pick up my daughter from daycare and drop her off at my girlfriend's house."

"No problem," Mitch said. "You look great."

"Thank you," she said. "You know your girl gotta make her presence known wherever she goes, cuz."

"You're definitely doing your thing," he said.

"Let me show you to your seats," the hostess said.

The hostess led them to a table by the window, and they sat down and opened their menus. The waitress promptly came by their table to see if they were ready to place their orders. She was a very attractive, brunette young lady, who could barely squeeze her big chest into the tiny Hooters t-shirt she was wearing.

"Hello, my name is Joan. Can I start you off with some drinks?"

"I'll have a Coke or Pespi," Tisha replied.

"And I'll have a Miller Draft," Mitch replied.

"We serve Pepsi, hon," the waitress corrected her.

"That's fine," Tisha said.

"Coming right up," the waitress said.

"You don't drink?" Mitch asked.

"I might drink some wine every now and then, but technically, I'm not old enough to drink yet," Tisha answered. "I have a fake ID in case someone tries to card me."

"Oh, yeah, that's right. You turn twenty-one in August, right?"

"Yep, August 21st, and I can't wait."

"Are you gonna throw a party?"

"Hell yeah, and you better come."

"Count me in."

"So, what have you been doing with yourself, Mitch? I heard your nightclub was still doing well, Mr. Big Time."

"Was doing well, Tish. I've been going through some serious stuff, but I'm gonna to be okay."

"What kind of serious stuff? Can I help?"

"I'm afraid not. See, right after Wes died, the IRS audited me and froze all my assets. I lost my job, my nightclub, and my house, and I've been living out of a suitcase ever since."

"Do you need some money?"

"Nah, Tish, I'm straight. They don't know about the loot I had stashed in my safe, and I still got almost two hundred grand left."

"Well then, can I have some money?"

"I see you got jokes."

"Yeah, plenty."

The waitress brought them their drinks and said, "Are you ready to order?"

"Yes, I'll have ten buffalo wings," Tisha replied.

"And you, sir?" the waitress asked.

"I'll have the same, but make mine barbeque instead," Mitch replied.

"Okay, I'll put that in for you," the waitress said. "Let me know if you need anything else."

"Thank you," Mitch said.

There was brief silence, and Tisha asked, "How's Kia? I miss my big sister."

"She's fine," Mitch answered. "She's just getting over a heartbreak, though."

"I'm sorry to hear that. I'm gonna give her a call tonight to see how she's doing."

"She'd like that. She's been going through a rough time lately...seems to be a lot of that going around these days."

"Tell me about it. I broke up with my daughter's father today."

"Is that why I saw you at the motel last night?"

"All in my business, huh?"

"I'm just saying, inquiring minds wanna know."

"Jimmy, my baby's daddy, wasn't giving me what I needed, so I dumped him. He got too comfortable, and he stopped doing what it took to get me in the first place."

"I understand, but are you sure you're leaving him for the right reasons? Sometimes, a person can do everything in their power to try to please you, but it's still not enough."

"Are you speaking from personal experience?"

"Yes, I am. My ex-wife Sandra was everything a man could want and then some, but I cheated on her anyway."

"I'm not judging you, but why did you do something so stupid, cuz?"

"Because I thought I could get away with it."

"But you didn't get away with it..."

"I *did* get away with it for almost ten years, but my dirt finally caught up with me."

"Sounds like you sincerely have regrets."

"I most definitely do, so do me a favor and make sure you're doing it for the right reasons."

"I'm in love with a married man, so how right can it be?"

"I can tell you from first-hand experience that it's probably not going to end well for you two. Just be careful, okay?"

"I am—I mean, we are. We've only been seeing each other for a couple of days."

"And that's why you broke up with Jimmy, right? The grass may seem greener, and sometimes, it is. But, there's always a flip side to the coin."

"Yeah, I know, but I also know how I feel. I never felt this way about anyone, Mitch."

"I can relate to that as well. I met the girl of my dreams last year, but she played me for a damn fool. She left me when things started going bad for me."

"So, she was only in it for the money, huh?"

"Absolutely, but I really thought we had more than a superficial romance."

"What's her name?"

"Brea Jones, and she's a recording artist, who's about to drop her first album."

"An R&B singer? Big mistake."

"Yes, she chose her career over me. But that's not why I'm mad at her."

"What could possibly be worse than that?"

"I found out she was indirectly involved the night my club got robbed and Wes got killed."

"Really? Did the police arrest her?"

"She didn't have anything to do with it, but she knew what was about to go down and said nothing. She chose to lie about it by faking an emergency, so I wouldn't be at the club when it got robbed."

"How do you know she telling the truth? We as women can be pretty conniving when we wanna be."

"I think I know her pretty well. I can tell when she's telling the truth most of the time, and I truly believe she thought she was doing what was best for me. I'd be dead if I would've been there with Wes that night."

"That's messed up. So, who were the people responsible? You said your ex knew about what was going down."

"Her twin sister, Bria, set me up by planting the guns in the men's bathroom the night before the robbery because we frisk everybody at the door."

"Is she locked up?"

"Can you believe she passed the polygraph? Now, I'm out here on my own trying to make stuff happen—trying to find the people responsible."

"My faith in the judicial system just went down a notch."

"And that's why I'm here, Tish. I know who killed Wes, and I'm going to make him suffer the consequences."

"You know who killed Wes?"

"Yeah, we used to be friends and were teammates in college. His name is Gary Maxwell, but everybody calls him Max."

Tisha's entire expression suddenly changed—it was like someone belted her in the stomach with a sledgehammer and made her torso cave in. She started hyperventilating uncontrollably, and

Mitch tried to comfort her.

"What's wrong?" Mitch asked with concern.

"I can't breathe," Tisha coughed. "Did you say *Max*?"

"Yeah, why?" Mitch asked, gently rubbing her back.

She paused for a moment, took a deep breath and said, "Max is the married man I've been messing around with..."

"Hell no, Tish! How is that possible?"

"I don't know..."

"You have to stay away from him. This guy is as shady as they come."

"You don't have to worry, Mitch. I promise I'm done with him."

"Where can I find him?"

"I thought you said for us to stay away from him."

"I meant *you*, not me. Where does he live?"

"Around the block from the Southern campus."

"Come on, take me there."

"What about the food?"

"Forget about the damn food. Come on. Let's go."

Mitch placed forty dollars on the table, and they left. Mitch stopped walking once they both stood a few yards from Tisha's car.

"On second thought, give me Max's address. I want to handle this alone."

"No, Mitch, Wes was my cousin too, so I'm going with you. I wanna see him face-to-face."

"I can't put you in harm's way. Max has proven himself to be a loose cannon, and this fool might try to pop off on me."

"I'm scared for you, Mitch..."

"Don't worry. I can handle myself."

Tisha reluctantly told Mitch where Max lived, and he scampered to his car and sped off toward the expressway while Tisha sat on the hood of her car and watched him leave the lot. The scene played out almost exactly like the recurring nightmare Mitch constantly relived for the past eight months—Tisha turned out to be the faceless, mystery woman in his dream, and the parking lot he would abruptly leave over and over again was Hooters. However, he would always wake up before he could see Max's face.

62

Tisha parked her car in front of her apartment and saw Jimmy's car was still there. She frowned, and she grabbed her purse before getting out. She took a deep breath and proceeded to walk toward the front door. A dark shadow appeared out of nowhere, and the mysterious figure tackled her to the ground.

"Get off me!" Tisha screamed. "What the hell are you doing?"

"You tried to steal my husband, you backstabbing tramp!" Jill shouted as she began to pummel Tisha's face.

"I'm sorry, Jill. Please stop hitting me!"

"Shut up, Tisha! I was your friend, and this is how you repay me?"

"I'm so sorry!"

Tisha somehow mustered the strength to wrestle Jill off her, and she slowly rose to her feet with a bloody nose and busted lip. Jill stood up and angrily looked Tisha in the eye.

"I see the way you look at him when you think nobody's watching," Jill said. "I'm not letting you or anybody else destroy my family."

"I don't want him, Jill," Tisha said.

"Yeah, right—I don't believe you."

"I said I'm done with him—did you know that your husband is a murderer?"

"Of course I know—what does it matter to you?"

"So, you know what he has done, and you're okay with that?"

"Done what?"

"Did you know he killed my cousin?"

"Who the hell is your cousin?"

"Your trifling husband robbed my cousins' nightclub, and he shot my cousin Wesley to death," Tisha said as she wiped tears and blood from her face.

"What the hell are you talking about?"

"Don't play dumb with me, heifer—you better hope my other cousin doesn't find him..."

"I had no idea Max killed your cousin, Wesley. We were just supposed to take the score and start our new life."

"So, my cousin was just a score to you?"

"Wait a minute, did you say Wesley was your cousin?"

"Yeah, so?"

"Who's your other cousin?"

"Your husband used to be friends with my cousin, Mitch Black."

"Wait a minute—I know Mitch, and he isn't like that. He's one of the nicest people I've ever met."

"That may be, but that still doesn't change the fact that he's on his way to your house right now to find Max and make him pay for what he's done to our family."

There was a long pause, and Jill broke the silence by saying, "I suggest you stay away from me and Melissa. Like me, she won't wanna have anything to do with you."

"She might not wanna have anything to do with you, either," Tisha countered. "I'll able to live with myself someday for what I've done, but can you, Jill?"

"I've gotta pick up my son—you better hope Max doesn't kill Mitch..."

"No, you better hope Mitch doesn't kill Max."

Jill pulled her phone out of her purse and hit Max's number.

"Call me back as soon as you get my message," she said.

Jill looked at Tisha with utter disdain and shook her head. Tisha returned Jill's stare with an equal look of displeasure before Jill got in her car and left. Tisha picked up her purse from the grass and went inside her apartment.

"Jimmy, are you in here?" Tisha asked. "I thought I made myself clear to you. James!"

She looked in their bedroom, and she looked in the guestroom. Still no sign of him. She then went to the bathroom to wipe off her face and found Jimmy sitting motionless in the tub with just his boxers on.

"Jimmy!" she screamed. "Oh my God, Nooooo! Aiyeeeee! Aiyeeeee!"

She saw an empty fifth of Crown Royal on the bathroom floor next to the tub, and she grabbed his wrist to check his pulse.

"Jimmy snap out of it!" she shouted as she repeatedly tapped his left cheek. "Come on, Jimmy. Stay with me!"

She could still feel a slight pulse, so she got her phone and quickly dialed 911.

"I need an ambulance right now, please," she said.

63

Mitch was close to Southern University's campus as he sped down Harding Drive and turned right at Scenic Avenue. He then made a quick right turn on Snipe Street and drove for a half a block before pulling up at Max's house. He sat in the car and waited for a brief moment, and as soon as he reached for the door, his cell phone rang.

"Ced?" Mitch asked. "I've been trying to reach you for weeks."

"Hey, Mitch," Cedric said. "We got him."

"You got who?"

"Gary Maxwell—he's looking down the barrel of a nine-millimeter right now as we speak. How fast can you get down here to Baton Rouge? I'll save him for you if you want."

"I'm already here, and I'm parked behind what appears to be your Lincoln Continental."

"Great, come on in and join the party."

Mitch got out of his car and walked toward the house. The door was unlocked, and he slowly walked inside and saw Max sitting in a chair bound by a rope with two massive human beings standing over him. Cedric stood on the opposite side of his henchmen in the living room area smoking a cigarette. The three of them had on business attire.

"Hey, Mitch, good to see you," Cedric said. "Want a cigarette?"

"Nah, I quit," Mitch answered. "I'm sorry I didn't dress for the occasion."

"Don't worry about it," Cedric said. "Do you have any last words, Gary?"

Mitch walked toward Max and punched him square in the jaw before saying, "I should blow your damn brains out right now!"

Max spat out some blood and said, "I deserved that, Black. I didn't know y'all owned that club. I swear I didn't know..."

"You didn't have to shoot him, Max! I thought we were friends, man!"

"We are friends, Black," Max pleaded. "I know what I did was foul, but I'm not that guy anymore. I've turned my whole life around for my son."

"Wes had a son, too, but now my little cousin is going to grow up without a father," Mitch said.

"If I had to do it over again, I wouldn't have shot Wes," Max said. "I had only a couple of seconds to react."

"I don't give a damn about what you're saying right now," Mitch said. "You-are-going-to-pay for killing Wes!"

"Enough with the talking, Mitch," Cedric said. "Are you gonna waste him or what?"

Jill barged in and saw Max bound to the chair with a gun to his head. She looked over at Mitch and then at Cedric before running toward Max, but one of Cedric's bodyguards grabbed her.

"Let go of me!" Jill shouted.

"Let her go, Stevens," Cedric said.

"What the hell is going on?" Jill asked after forcefully jerking her shoulders from Stevens' grasp.

"You tell me," Mitch answered. "Why did you all rob my damn club? I don't believe one word coming out of Max's mouth right now."

"I didn't know Gary was going to kill your cousin, Mitch," Jill said. "I just found out what happened from your other cousin, Tisha."

"Yeah, and she told me what was going on between her and Max," Mitch said. "Did you know about them?"

"Yeah, I just found out about that, too," Jill answered, looking angrily over at Max.

"Sounds like you have a lot going on here, Gary," Cedric said. "Why don't you just let me put you out of your misery, homeboy?"

"Tyrone is gonna make you pay if you kill me, Cedric," Max said.

"No, Gary, I'm afraid not," Cedric said. "You see, I turned the lights out on your entire crew—Quentin, Norris, and Tyrone are all dead. You're the last man standing."

Mitch pulled out his gun and aimed it at Max's head. He then looked at Jill's face and saw the horror in her eyes.

"Come on Mitch, do it!" Cedric shouted. "It's your call—he can live, or he can die. It's all on you Mitch—my word is bond."

The look on Jill's face rattled Mitch's spirit, and because of this, he lowered his gun and tucked it back in his pants. Jill sighed in relief.

"I can't go out like that," Mitch said. "You aren't worth it, Max."

"Are you sure, Mitch?" Cedric asked.

"Yeah, I'm sure, Ced," Mitch answered. "Judgment will come upon him in some form or fashion, but I'm not the judge, jury, or executioner. Killing him won't bring Wes back or make me feel any better."

"Come on, men. We're out," Cedric said. "And let me give you a word of advice, Gary—don't ever step foot in Chicago again, or all bets are off."

"Take care of yourself, Ced," Mitch said.

"You, too, little brother," Cedric said.

Cedric and his henchmen left Max's house, and Jill quickly untied Max from the chair before tightly embracing him. Mitch then motioned toward the front door.

"Mitch wait," Jill called out to him.

"What is it, Jill?" Mitch asked, turning around to face the two of them.

"Thank you," she said.

"I did it for you, Jill," Mitch said.

"Yeah, thank you, bruh," Max said.

"I forgive you Max," Mitch said, "but things between us will never be the same."

He nodded at Max, and Max nodded back as there were no more words to say between them. He then walked out of the house and wasted no time driving off. Chicago was roughly fifteen hours away, and he planned on only stopping for gas and snacks—anxious to get home and get his life back on track with no distractions hindering him.

Mitch decided to take a step back and let the due process of law run its natural course as he headed east on Interstate 12. He knew Max and Bria were the only two people still alive who directly had a hand in Wesley's death, but he also knew that he didn't have any concrete proof to implicate them. However, if the police were lucky enough to come up with any shred of evidence—a fingerprint, a witness to link either one of them to the murder, or a confession—he wouldn't hesitate to testify against them.

Mitch couldn't pull the trigger on Max after seeing the anguish on Jill's face—the feelings of remorse and guilt for aiding and abetting Max in all his schemes and turning a blind eye to them had finally resonated with her. Mitch also knew that Jill's presence saved him, as well as Max, because killing his former best friend in front of her in cold blood would probably lead to life in prison without the possibly of parole in Angola.

He felt like a huge weight had been lifted off his shoulders—he was free from the pressures of his financial woes, free from the stress of a broken marriage, free from his philandering ways, and most of all, free from carrying the burden of guilt from Wesley's murder. He felt completely free for the first time in his life.

Moments later, a familiar angelic voice was faintly playing on the radio as Mitch was approaching the I-12/I-55 split, so he turned up the volume and listened attentively to the song. He laughed out loud after realizing the song was Brea's new hit single, and the lyrics were about him.

"This woman really thinks I'm broke," he said.

Made in the USA
Middletown, DE
31 July 2019